Bad Boys' Pranks

Weitere Storys

www.sprachkrimis.de

Weitere Storys im Internet!

1. *Scanne den QR-Code auf dem Buch-Cover oder auf dieser Seite mit deinem Smartphone ein.*

   Dafür benötigt dein Gerät einen QR-Code-Scanner. Dieser ist entweder vorinstalliert oder kann als kostenlose App von zahlreichen Anbietern heruntergeladen werden.

2. *Mithilfe des QR-Codes gelangst du direkt auf die Website unserer Sprachkrimireihe. Natürlich kannst du auch ohne Smartphone auf die Website gelangen, indem du folgende Webadresse eingibst:*

   www.sprachkrimis.de

3. *Auf der Website findest du einen spannenden Kurzkrimi in englischer Sprache und Übungen dazu.*

Bad Boys' Pranks

Autorin: Ulrike Rudolph
Muttersprachliches Korrektorat:
Context Gesellschaft für Sprachen- und Mediendienste mbH
Satz: Noch & Noch
Covergestaltung: Marlies Müller
Coverillustration: Hauke Kock

Gesamtherstellung: Tandem Verlag GmbH

ISBN 978-3-8427-0833-4

www.tandem-verlag.de

Prologue

Don't move! Breathe slowly, so they can't see that you still feel the pain. Pretend to have lost consciousness[1]. Don't feel for your ribs, even if they burn like fire.

Are those boys still there? Is there any shuffling[2] of feet?

There is a rhythm, strong and fast. But it is not outside; it is in my body, beating painfully against my chest[3] and eardrums[4] from the inside. Apart from that it is quiet. It seems to be over. Doesn't it?

Don't move. Breathe slowly.

The ground I'm lying on feels hard and uneven. The concrete paving slab[5] presses my elbow into my side. Exactly the spot where that boy's black leather shoe hit me, though I was already lying on the street. It would help a lot if I could move a bit.

Are they gone?

How long have I been lying here without being beaten and kicked?

There must have been four or five of them. They met me unprepared when I walked around the corner. Was he with them? Was it all a joke for him?

It is quiet now. I'm cold. And there is no jacket left, nothing to cover my bruised[6], bare arms.

I'll have to hurry home and take care that nobody sees me. They would start asking questions.

But the last thing I need right now is curious[7] people.

The only thing I need at the moment is a hot tub and a wealthy[8] friend.

Or a bank robbery.

1 consciousness – Bewusstsein 2 to shuffle – schlurfen 3 chest – Brustkorb 4 eardrum – Trommelfell
5 concrete paving slab – Betonfußwegplatte 6 bruised – blau vom Bluterguss 7 curious – neugierig
8 wealthy – wohlhabend

Chapter 1

"What the heck[1] ..."

Sandra Dingles, the headmistress[2] of Looe Comprehensive School pushed back her chair and stood up. The typewritten sheet of paper in her right hand trembled.

Her hands never trembled, neither when she was making a speech in front of hundreds of students and parents, nor in a council meeting[3] when she had to fight against the closedown[4] of her school and its integration into the bigger community school in Liskeard. It was not her fault that many families had left Cornwall because of the bad employment market[5] in this part of the country. Those children who had stayed here needed a school in the neighbourhood.

And what her children needed, apart from a school in their direct neighbourhood, was definitely not this kind of threatening letter[6], which made her hand tremble this morning as if she was a hundred years old. But that was exactly how she felt.

"May I have your attention please," she shouted into the crowd of busy teachers in the staffroom[7].

"Attention please!"

Sandra cleared her throat[8] and put the letter onto her desk. The others must not see her hand tremble.

"I'm afraid we have a situation."

She tapped the letter with her finger. When she was sure that the last conversation had stopped and she had the undivided[9] attention of her staff, she sat down and picked up the letter. But she rested her elbows on the table to steady herself.

"As in 'Houston, we have a situation' at the explosion of an oxygen tank on Apollo 13?" the history teacher asked.

1 what the heck – was zum Teufel 2 headmistress – Direktorin 3 council meeting – Ratsversammlung 4 closedown – Schließung 5 employment market – Stellenmarkt 6 threatening letter – Drohbrief 7 staffroom – Lehrerzimmer 8 to clear one's throat – sich räuspern 9 undivided – ungeteilt

Exercise 1

Zeitreise: Setze die folgenden Verben ins Präsenz.

1. *written* ________________
2. *left* ________________
3. *read* ________________

"Well, pretty much like that," Sandra said and frowned[10]. "I only hope that we can avoid[11] the explosion."

As all eyes rested on her, Sandra read the letter aloud.

"I will cause you and everybody at your school real trouble, bloody trouble. On the 16th of June. You will repent[12]."

There was silence. You could have heard a pin drop. After a moment somebody started laughing.

Exercise 2

Wessen? Setze die folgenden Begriffe in den Genitiv.

1. *the headmistress* ________________
2. *the children* ________________
3. *her house* ________________

"It must be a joke, mustn't it?", somebody said. But he didn't sound too convinced[13].

10 to frown – die Stirn runzeln 11 to avoid – verhindern 12 to repent – Buße tun, bereuen 13 convinced – überzeugt

"They can't mean it," a female voice could be heard, "Not in the British countryside."

All of a sudden everybody started talking with their neighbours until Sandra called their attention again.

Exercise 3

Viele: Bilde den Plural der folgenden Substantive.

1. *child* ____________________
2. *information* ____________________
3. *teacher* ____________________

"I don't think this is really – well – dangerous, you know. Not so serious that we should call the police. That would only support those in the community who want to close us down – you understand. To me it sounds like one of those bad boys' pranks we all know so well. But on the other hand we'll have to take steps to make sure that nobody has gone insane[14] and tries to hurt anybody."

Many heads nodded[15].

"Exactly!"

"Aye ..."

"Hear, hear!"

"That's right!"

Sandra put the letter back on the desk.

"Well then ... let's get everything organised before the kids come in."

14 to go insane – durchdrehen 15 to nod – nicken

Chapter 2

Rebecca Higgin's mother Leonora slowed down her taxi in front of a traffic light and turned her head to face her daughter, who was sitting in the left-hand back seat.

"Well, I hope you will do better in today's test than in the last one," Leonora said with a sigh[1]. Your new hairdo[2] is nice. It suits you[3] short!"

Becca's grandmother Georgina looked at Becca from the right-hand back seat with a smile. "And who are you, my dear?"

"I'm Becca, your granddaughter, Granny. Remember? Your bedroom is next to mine. And by the way," Becca turned to her mother behind the steering wheel, "My last test was the second-best in the class, so what are you on about?"

Her mother drove on.

"Where are we going? Have the monkeys been fed[4] yet?" Georgina asked. Her face showed an expression of deep concern.

"Yes, everything is fine, mother, all the animals are well and we are on our way to Brighton, where the Circus will stay for two whole weeks and perform every afternoon and night. But right now you have to be quiet, dear. The lions are very restless!"

Georgina sucked in air through her teeth and pressed her lips together.

Exercise 4

Satzsalat: Bringe die Wörter in die richtige Reihenfolge.

her letter tapped she with finger the.

1 sigh – Seufzer 2 hairdo – Haarschnitt 3 to suit s.b. – jmd. gut stehen 4 feed – füttern

Becca knew that her grandmother would not say a word for quite a while. Mentioning the lions was the best way to silence her, especially when her mother Leonora had passengers. In the summertime, like now in June, her mother was quite busy with her taxi business. And it sometimes disturbed[5] the passengers when they saw the old lady sitting in the back seat. But this was the only possible way to keep Granny from running away to some faraway Circus only she could see.

Sometimes Becca and her mother wished they could afford[6] a care home for Georgina, but that was far too expensive[7] as Leonora's income[8] was only good in summer. But in the wintertime, with no tourists in the little town of Looe on the South Eastern Cornwall coast, she had little to do and time enough to take care of Grandma.

Exercise 5

Gewusst, was: Verbinde die englischen Sprichwörter *(idioms)* mit der richtigen deutschen Übersetzung.

In for a penny, in for a pound.	*sich nach der Decke strecken*
All good things come in threes.	*Wer A sagt, muss auch B sagen.*
to make ends meet	*Aller guten Dinge sind drei.*

Georgina had grown up as the daughter of two animal tamers[9], the famous Martins from Newcastle. She had inherited[10] her parents' passion for all kinds of animals. And for travelling. So the taxi business had turned out to be quite a good way to keep Georgina under control when she developed Alzheimer's disease several years ago.

5 to disturb – stören 6 to afford – sich leisten 7 expensive – kostspielig 8 income – Einkommen 9 animal tamer – Dompteur 10 to inherit – erben

Becca took her grandmother's hand and squeezed[11] it lightly.

"Everything's fine," she said, and Georgina nodded.

Leonora pulled the taxi into a parking space in front of the Looe Comprehensive School to let Becca out.

"Do your best, sweetheart," she said.

Exercise 6

Besserwisser: Steigere die folgenden Adjektive.

1. *good,* ____________________, ____________________
2. *bad,* ____________________, ____________________
3. *light,* ____________________, ____________________

And when Becca turned around to walk up to the school entrance she heard one of her grandmother's famous last anchors in her waters of forgetfulness[12]:

"Every cloud has a silver lining[13] …"

11 to squeeze – drücken 12 waters of forgetfulness – das Vergessen 13 every cloud has a silver lining – es gibt immer einen Silberstreifen am Horizont

Chapter 3

"Is everybody at his or her post[1]?" Sandra Dingles asked and looked around.

Half of the staff was outside at the school entrance, checking the students' bags and jackets for weapons or other dangerous items which might be used to cause the announced trouble.

Some teachers were still discussing the letter.

The mouse-like voice of Jenny Peters, the history teacher, was squeaking: "There must be a motive, a reason for the letter. Wait and see …"

Exercise 7

Zeitreise: Setze die Verben in die einfache Vergangenheit (*past tense*, z. B. *went*)!

1. *Becca (knows) ________________ her grandmother.*
2. *Ms Dingles (is) ________________ very concerned.*
3. *Becca's grandma (likes) ________________ the circus.*

Sandra silently[2] agreed with the history teacher. Who could have a motive?

There were several final tests for this term[3], as well as A-level exams scheduled[4] for today, but would that be a motive for such a threat? To mess up the whole routine of her school? With all the possible consequences for the evildoer[5] when his or her identity was discovered?

1 to be at one's post – auf seinem Posten sein 2 silently – im Stillen 3 term – Halbjahr 4 to be scheduled – fällig sein 5 evildoer – Übeltäter

Exercise 8

Parallelwelten: Finde die Gegenteilpaare und verbinde sie mit Strichen.

1. *admit*	*above*
2. *annoy*	*deny*
3. *below*	*please*

"I don't want to put the blame on anybody," the history teacher went on in a lower voice. But Sandra could hear her. Jenny Peters pulled her skirt down. It was too short, as usual. She was talking with Jack Jacobs, the student teacher. He must be 10 years younger than her. A circumstance that did not keep her from shaking her grey hair like a singer on stage and staring at him with a look she probably found seductive[6].

"Philippa Shneiders," she continued. "You know? Her father puts a lot of pressure on her, because she is supposed[7] to go to St. Andrews on a scholarship[8] one day. He went there, and today he is a famous lawyer. Anyhow. She will need very good A-level results. And the exam today – well, modern history is not exactly her hobbyhorse[9], to put it mildly[10]."

"I know Philippa and her problems," the student teacher replied. The kids called him "Jayjay" like a double stupid jaybird. "But why should it be her and nobody else? There are many others who might have a motive for such a letter and the wish for a day off[11] – or even want to see the school closed permanently."

6 seductive – verführerisch 7 to be supposed to – vorgesehen sein für 8 scholarship – Stipendium 9 hobbyhorse – Steckenpferd 10 to put sth. mildly – milde ausdrücken 11 a day off – ein freier Tag

Exercise 9

Lückenfüller: Setze die richtigen Präpositionen ein!

1. *Leonora pulled the taxi ________________ a parking space.*
2. *I don't want to put the blame ________________ anybody.*
3. *The taxi business turned ________________ to be quite good.*

Yes, Sandra thought, how true. And you, Jayjay – I mean, Jacobs – with your absolute absence[12] of educational competence and your lack of the slightest[13] talent for the profession of a teacher, so much so that even students realise it, are definitely among those with a very strong motive. We will have to cancel your teaching exam today too.

Exercise 10

Buchstabensalat: Sortiere die Buchstaben so, dass sinnvolle Wörter entstehen!

1. *cadeutnalio* ________________
2. *obsheboryh* ________________
3. *shiplacorsh* ________________

Sandra felt sick at the thought of calling the invigilator[14] and explaining why they had to postpone Jack Jacobs' demonstration lesson. But the risk that one of the kids would blow the whistle[15] on the real reason, the threatening letter, for this act of postpone-

12 absence – Abwesenheit 13 slight – gering 14 invigilator – Aufsicht 15 to blow the whistle – verraten

ment[16] was far too high, especially on the very day all this has happened.

How should she, as the headmistress, explain why they hadn't called the police? Even if they didn't find any real weapons, as Sandra had hoped. The decreasing[17] number of students would surely not be accepted as an explanation.

At this thought the staffroom door swung open with a bang and Donald, the PE teacher[18], rushed in with his skinny bare legs, waving a knife through the air like a tennis racket.

Exercise 11

Zeitreise: Setze die Verben ins Perfekt (*present perfect,* z.B. *has gone*)!

1. *When Becca arrives at school, Helen (go)* ________________ *inside.*
2. *When Ms Dingles starts speaking, everybody (stop)* ________________ *talking.*
3. *When Becca leaves the taxi, her Grandma (fall)* ________________ *asleep.*

"Only small weapons so far," he exclaimed, "or rather cutlery[19], for buttering toast or, in the most dangerous case, for peeling apples and oranges".

That man always belittles[20] problems, Sandra thought, *no matter how serious they are!*

But they had not yet reached the end of their investigations.

16 postponement – Aufschub 17 to decrease – zurückgehen 18 PE – (physical education) teacher – Sportlehrer 19 cutlery – Besteck 20 to belittle – verniedlichen

Chapter 4

When Becca approached the steps in front of the school building she noticed the queue. A large group of youngsters was waiting to get in, at least 20 to 30 students. What was going on here? Nobody would want to queue in front of a school! And nobody ever had before.

She shifted her school bag further under her arm and looked around. Something was wrong, something she had not expected.

"Hi Becca! Come here!"

Helen Albright, her best mate[1], was waving at her.

Helen was close to the entrance. Becca exhaled. Only now she realised that she had held her breath.

She moved forward to get to Helen's side. But then she saw them. Teachers, on both sides of the three entrance doors. And there were more inside the building, right behind the doors.

What the hell ...?

Helen called her name again. Then she waved both hands to make Becca come.

"I'm almost there!"

Now Helen had to turn around as the maths teacher talked to her. She stepped forward and took her bag from her shoulder. Becca could see how Helen's long blonde hair fell over her arms as she bent forward. What did she do? Becca could only see her back. The teacher smiled at Helen. That was what everybody did when Helen appeared: smile and do what she wanted.

Turn around, Helen, Becca thought. Show me what is going on here!

Helen was gone, vanished behind the doors. Some other students followed her.

1 mate – Kumpel

Exercise 12

Betrüger: Finde die falsche Übersetzung des Sprichwortes.

1. *Don't count your chickens before they've hatched.* — *Man soll das Fell des Bären nicht verteilen, bevor man ihn erlegt hat.*
2. *Better safe than sorry.* — *Doppelt hält besser.*
3. *to be the cock of the walk* — *der Hahn auf dem Laufsteg sein*

Becca stayed where she was. She needed to find out what was happening. She felt her fists clench[2] on her bag.

Relax, calm down, she said to herself. But she could not free from the enormous tension she felt in her whole body. She nervously groped her neck and stretched it.

Exercise 13

Zeitreise: Setze die Verben in die Zukunftsform (*future*, z.B. *will go*)!

1. *Sandra (cancel) ________________ Jacob's exam.*
2. *Helen (call) ________________ Becca after school.*
3. *Becca (face) ________________ the teacher's call.*

Philippa Shneiders was next. She was not a close friend of Becca's, but a minute ago Philippa had looked at her and made a funny face which Becca could not interpret.

Philippa stepped aside from the teacher and stopped. Now

2 to clench – sich verkrampfen

Becca could see how the teacher opened Philippa's backpack and put his hand inside. He took some books out and used his other hand to move some stuff inside the backpack from one side to the other. Then he put the books back in and waved Philly to go through.

He looked at Becca and frowned.

"Rebecca Higgins, come on!"

No way! Becca thought.

Exercise 14

Betrüger: Finde den Fehler in einem der folgenden Sätze.

1. *Helen Albright, her best mate, was waving at Becca.*
2. *What was going on here?*
3. *Becca stayed where she were.*

She turned around. She had to leave this place immediately or her cunning[3] plan would explode in her face. And that might hurt not only her, but others too.

3 cunning – gerissen, durchtrieben

Chapter 5

The Western Looe harbour pier was dozing[1] in the sun after the busy early morning activities. The smell of fish and seaweed[2] was still hanging over the deserted pavement. Some empty plastic containers were leaning against the small harbour houses waiting for their evening and night mission. Only a few kids were lying on their bellies putting their crab[3] fishing nets into the shallow[4] water. Their parents were sitting on the wooden benches with their eyes closed, their faces turned towards the sun.

Exercise 15

Verbbeuger: Ergänze die fehlenden Konjunktionsformen der folgenden Verben (z.B. *go, went, gone*)!

1. *to lie,* ____________________, ____________________
2. *to sit,* ____________________, ____________________
3. *to hang,* ____________________, ____________________

Dash Hunter was wondering what would happen if one of the kids fell into the water. Would anybody but him notice? Would the sound of the splash[5] caused by a falling kid in such shallow water be loud enough to warn the parents? Or would they be too busy sun-worshipping?

"Hey, sonny[6], be careful," Dash called towards a boy who was leaning far over the pier to get his net into the water. "The edge is slippery!"

1 to doze – dösen 2 seaweed – Seetang 3 crab – Taschenkrebs 4 shallow – seicht 5 splash – Schwall
6 sonny – Kleiner

Exercise 16

Lückenfüller: Ergänze das fehlende Wort!

1. *Becca could not free herself from the enormous tension she felt in her whole ________________.*
2. *The teacher put the books ________________ in the backpack and waved Philly to go through.*
3. *The Western Looe harbour pier was ________________ in the sun after the busy early morning activities.*

Ah! Now the mothers on their benches opened their eyes. And one father got up and pulled his little girl away from the edge. She cried out and reached out for her yellow bucket. There were several crabs in it already; the famous Looe family lunch was saved for today.

Exercise 17

Besserwisser: Welche der folgenden Aussagen ist falsch?

1. *Becca's mother is a taxi driver.*
2. *Helen Albright is Becca's best friend.*
3. *Jack Jacobs is the school caretaker.*

Dash turned away. His family had never been able to go on holiday, in common with most Cornish people apart from the handful who did not earn their living through tourism.

Dash had had enough of the local crab sandwiches for a lifetime!

He moved forward to the steps leading down to the water. The little open foot passenger ferry from the Eastern bank[7] of the Looe River was approaching. Dash looked around and was relieved[8] that he was alone – apart from those tourists who didn't really count.

He hurried down the steep steps. As the small boat arrived he took the wet rope[9] from Andrew's, the ferryman's hand, tied it down[10] on the iron handrail and reached out his hand to help old Mrs Fletcher disembark[11] safely.

Exercise 18

Hauptsache: Unterstreiche die Substantive (keine Namen!) im vorigen Absatz und setze sie in den Plural oder Singular.

"Thank you, Dashiel," she said in her soft voice. "Your mother would be proud of you if she could see you now!"

You bet, Dash thought, she really would. Helping old ladies across the river had always been his mother's favourite career aspiration[12] for her only son.

"You're welcome, Mrs Fletcher," Dash said with a smile. "And how's your arthritis today?"

"I'm just on my way to see the doctor. It's not getting any better."

"Ah, that's too bad. Good luck with the doctor. And be careful on the steps. They are still wet and really slippery from the flood. Hold on tight to the handrail!"

7 bank – Ufer 8 relieved – erleichtert 9 rope – Tau 10 to tie down – festzurren 11 to disembark – aussteigen (Schiff), anlanden 12 career aspiration – Berufswunsch

Exercise 19

Lückenfüller: Ergänze das fehlende Wort und übertrage das Sprichwort ins Deutsche.

1. *My* ________________ *stood on end.*

   ____

2. *I wouldn't want to be in her* ________________.

   ____

3. *That's* ________________ *hat.*

   ____

Dash watched the old lady climbing up the steps. She looked weak and poorly[13]. He held back the two other passengers on the boat – tourists, obviously, judging by their fancy clothing. They could wait until the old girl had reached the top without the haste and pressure of somebody following right behind her. For the old people from Looe this ferry was still the most popular and quickest shortcut from one bank of the river to the other. They ignored the bridge which crossed the river only a few hundred metres away, although that bridge had been built by their own great-grandfathers. The old locals[14] considered the bridge a touristy device. They only used it when they had to take the bus or taxi or – if they had one – a car to get from the suburbs[15] of West Looe into the old town of East Looe, where they could get everything they needed.

Dash reached out for the lady tourist's arm and helped her onto the jetty[16]. Her husband followed on his own.

13 poorly – schlecht 14 local – Ortsansässiger 15 suburb – Vorort 16 jetty – Anleger

Exercise 20

Strippenzieher: Verbinde die folgenden *phrasal verbs* (Verb mit Partikel) mit der richtigen deutschen Übersetzung.

look up	*sich freuen*
look forward	*sich streiten/ausfallen*
look for	*nachschlagen*
fall out	*verdeutlichen*
get across	*suchen*

The ferry crossed the river from sunrise until midnight. It was still a profitable little enterprise and Dash was happy that Andrew had agreed to give him a chance to learn the business.

When both tourists had left the staircase, Dash jumped into the ferry.

Exercise 21

„Am Lesen sein“: Setze die folgenden Verben in die Verlaufsform.

1. *The teachers (looked) ________________ for weapons in the students backpacks.*
2. *Helen (chased) ________________ Becca all day long.*
3. *Becca (kept) ________________ out of her best friend's reach.*

"Well done, boy," Andrew said. His light blue eyes were shining like jewels. They made a nice contrast to the dark potato-like nose in his sunburnt face. Andrew was almost 70 and dreamed of retiring[17].

"Now let's see how you handle this old barge[18]. My wife will be happy to have me on hand to work in the garden every other day[19] if you do well."

Dash started the machine and turned the ferry carefully, when he heard a familiar voice from the pier.

"Hey, Hunter, finally found your ultimate vocation[20]? Your mother would be proud if she could see you now!"

Dash did not look up. He just murmured "Get lost[21], Jamie Dagger, get lost."

17 to retire – sich zur Ruhe setzen 18 barge – Barkasse 19 every other day – alle zwei Tage 20 vocation – Berufung 21 to get lost (colloquial/coll.) – Leine ziehen (umgangssprachlich/ugs.)

Chapter 6

"Well, young lady?" Ms Dingles asked.

The wristwatch on the headmistress's desk seemed to have a life of its own. As if it attracted everybody's attention in the office.

Exercise 22

Was wäre, wenn: Ergänze die fehlenden Verbformen in den folgenden If-Sätzen (Typ 1).

1. *If Dash gets the job, Jamie (kid) ________________ him.*
2. *If Ms Dingles keeps the watch, Becca (be) ________________ in trouble.*
3. *If Becca's grandma stays in the car, Becca (go out) ________________ at night.*

Becca felt her face still glowing as if the watch was sending out hot rays. Which was nonsense, of course.

She pulled in her breath and swallowed. She had been thinking of an explanation for that watch since the old geography teacher had found it in her bag. There had been no escape; he had just been too quick, holding her back from leaving, grabbing her arm and pulling her into his investigation area behind the entrance door.

"I found this watch," Becca finally said. She looked at her fingers and tried to keep them from moving, which was not so easy.

"I found it yesterday. I was going to take it to the lost property office[1] after school today."

"Really?" Ms Dingles snarled[2]. She didn't look convinced. "And where did you find it?"

Why didn't she just stop asking? Had they been searching all the students because they had been looking for this watch? But wouldn't Helen have called her in that case?

Exercise 23

Just do it: Unterstreiche die Verben und Hilfsverben im vorigen Absatz und konjugiere sie durch.

"I found it on the bridge, on my way home. Somebody must have lost it."

Exercise 24

Können und dürfen: Übersetze die folgenden Sätze und verwende *to be able to* oder *to be allowed to*.

1. *Becca kann das Geld nicht bezahlen.*

   ____

2. *Helen kann nicht alleine zum Festival fahren.*

   ____

3. *Die alte Dame kann die Treppe nicht schneller hinaufgehen.*

   ____

1 lost property office – Fundbüro 2 to snarl – knurren

"You know that this is a very expensive watch, don't you?"

Of course I do, otherwise this wouldn't make any sense, Becca thought. What she said was: "Oh! I thought it was only an old-fashioned[3] wristwatch an old lady tourist might have lost. I still wanted to give it back, you know. Sentimental value[4]. But if it's valuable, somebody will really miss it. So it's even more important you give it back to me, so I can get it on its way to its rightful owner."

Becca looked up into the head's face. But as she had expected, Ms Dingles didn't swallow it[5].

Exercise 25

Zukunftsmusik: Bilde die Zukunftsform, die eine feste Absicht ausdrückt oder unmittelbar bevorsteht (mit *going to*).

1. *Dash startet gleich die Maschine des Bootes.*

   ____

2. *Ms Dingles wird Beccas Mutter informieren.*

   ____

3. *Helen wird sich um Beccas Probleme kümmern.*

   ____

"This is a Cartier wristwatch, worth more than six thousand pounds. It would be irresponsible to leave it in a schoolgirl's hands. You might get robbed[6], for one thing. No, Rebecca, I'll take care of the watch. And I want to talk to your mother."

3 old-fashioned – altmodisch 4 sentimental value – Erinnerungswert 5 to swallow it – den Haken schlucken
6 to rob – ausrauben

That was the last thing Becca needed.

"My mother is on a trip to London, some businessman from Truro booked her for the whole week. She won't be back until next Monday."

Ms Dingles raised her eyebrows and then she looked at Becca through half-closed eyes.

Exercise 26

Was wäre, wenn: Ergänze die fehlenden Verbformen in den folgenden If-Sätzen (Typ 2).

1. *If Becca's grandma was well, Becca (leave) ________________ her alone.*
2. *If Jack Jacobs was a good teacher, the kids (like) ________________ him.*
3. *If Leonora was younger, she (move) ________________ to London to attend a further education programme for a new profession.*

"Well, in that case you are on your own? Is that what you are trying to say? A 14-year-old all on her own over the weekend?"

"N-no," Becca stammered[7]. "My grandmother is with me, I'm not alone!"

"Okay then. Let's get down to business."

The head looked at Becca sceptically, but she waved her hands to indicate to the other teachers that they could leave her office.

"And you, young lady, will get a letter for your mother. I'll write it right now. We have to talk."

7 to stammer – stammeln

Chapter 7

Sandra sealed the envelope and looked at Rebecca Higgins.

Who the heck is that young lady texting right in front of me? she thought.

Rebecca was waiting for the letter, but she did not appear too comfortable[1]. She seemed nervous as she pressed the buttons on her mobile phone.

Was she texting her mother? Or somebody else outside school? Maybe a boyfriend, one of the poor unemployed youths of Looe? Who were responsible for the graffiti on the school walls and for many fake phone calls about fire exercises and other bad boys' pranks? One of those guys, who always meant trouble? That would not surprise her.

Rebecca had changed over the last year, since her father had left the family. She had withdrawn from her former schoolmates and her results had worsened[2] a bit. Sandra and her staff had talked about Rebecca and her family[3] situation several times. Without any results. So far[4]. But if she had stolen this watch, which was highly likely[5], because tourists usually didn't wear such high-priced jewellery while travelling, that would change a lot.

At least she had nothing to do with the threatening letter, which had turned out to be just another bad boys' prank. They had not found any weapons, and nothing had happened. Apart from postponing tests …

Sandra cleared her throat[6].

Rebecca looked up from her mobile and put it into her trousers.

"Yes?"

1 comfortable – behaglich 2 to worsen – verschlechtern 3 family – familiär 4 so far – bis jetzt 5 likely – anzunehmen 6 to clear one's throat – sich räuspern

Exercise 27

Nicht dürfen: Übersetze die folgenden Sätze.

1. *Helen darf die Schule nicht verlassen.*

   ____

   ____

2. *Ms Dingles darf nicht über den Drohbrief reden.*

   ____

   ____

3. *Dash darf nicht zeigen, dass er verärgert ist.*

   ____

   ____

"Your boyfriend?"

"Yes. No. I mean …"

Rebecca's voice drifted away and she looked down at the floor instead of answering the question. Sandra waited another minute, but the student did not look up. In the end she handed over the letter and said: "I want to see your mother next week. Tell her to call me to make an appointment[7]. And if there is anything you want to tell me …?"

Rebecca shook her head, took the letter and left the office without looking back.

7 appointment – Termin

Exercise 28

Nicht müssen: Bilde die Verneinung der folgenden Sätze.

1. *The teachers must search the students.*

   ____

2. *The students must show them their backpacks.*

   ____

3. *The headmistress must report the threatening letter.*

   ____

Chapter 8

After school Becca hurried to follow Philippa outside. Becca had managed to stay out of Helen's way all day and didn't want to talk to her now.

"Tell me the truth," she said to Philippa. She heard her own voice tremble. "Did you write that bloody letter?"

"You're nuts[1], Rebecca, why should I? We'll write that test next week, won't we? So what? But what about you? What did the head want from you? Are you sure you're not in any trouble yourself? And trying to put the blame on me? Like those guys always do when people find out about their pranks? So what did you do?"

"N-nothing! I was just thinking ..." Becca replied. Her stomach was aching and her hands wet. Why did Philly have to mention those boys?

Philippa gave up waiting for Becca's reply. She shook her head and ran down the steps to jump into her father's SUV. Becca could see his golf equipment in the rear.

"Hey, Becca, wait for me!"

Helen!

Becca moved quickly down the steps. "I'm in a hurry, call you later, okay?" she shouted backwards over her shoulder and rushed on.

Her mother would turn around the corner any minute. Becca had to stop her before any of the teachers saw the taxi and realised that Becca had lied about her mother, that she had not left for London.

1 nuts (coll.) – bekloppt

Exercise 29

Müssen: Setze die korrekte Form von *must* oder *have to* in den folgenden Sätzen ein.

1. *Becca ________________ hurry up.*
2. *Students ________________ support their friends.*
3. *Grandma Georgina ________________ take her Alzheimer's medicine.*

Becca's heart was beating hard, from running and from all the excitement. But when she hurried around the corner of the red-brick building she did not see her mother's taxi. Nor the Looe bridge. She bumped right into the local gang of unemployed boys.

Their leader, Jamie Dagger, caught her in his arms. But Becca did not feel saved from falling. She felt her heart stop beating.

"There you are, beautiful! Earlier than expected. That's good. How are your bruises today?" Jamie turned Becca's arm and dramatically pushed up her sleeves to inspect her arm. His grip hurt.

The other guys grinned at Becca. She could not see all their faces. Was he among them?

"We better protect you from falling – and any other harm[2] that might come your way," Jamie whispered into Becca's ear.

Becca swallowed and looked at her feet. Despite the afternoon sun she was freezing. How should she explain that she didn't have the money? That the watch was gone and there was no chance to get it back? Would these guys listen to her? Or would they just beat her up?

2 harm – Schaden, Leid

Exercise 30

Besserwisser: Übersetze und erkläre, was die Sprichwörter bedeuten.

1. *to be on cloud nine*

   ____

2. *The apple doesn't fall far from the tree.*

   ____

3. *to sail close to the wind*

   ____

"I had an expensive watch," she started and looked up. There were five of them, she counted. And Dash was not with them.

"Right. And?" Jamie said. He was wearing her blue leather jacket, perhaps to hurt her feelings even more.

"I wanted to sell it this afternoon. But the head took it and kept it. So – there is no watch at the moment."

Exercise 31

Fundstücke: Finde im Anfang des Kapitels die englischen Entsprechungen zu diesen Sätzen und unterstreiche sie.

1. *Sie hörte, wie ihre Stimme zitterte.*
2. *Becca rannte die Stufen herunter.*
3. *Was machen heute deine blauen Flecke?*

She looked into Jamie's eyes. But there was no response, no reaction to her story. His gaze[3] was empty, his grey eyes like frozen water.

One of the guys behind him started thumping one of his hands into the open palm of the other.

Becca hugged her bag closer, and covered her belly with it. "I'm sorry, but ..."

"Are you telling me that you haven't got the money?"

"No, yes, I mean ... couldn't you wait a few days?"

"Wait for what?" Jamie came closer.

"We are not used to waiting. You get the money by tomorrow night. Ten o'clock. Or we will ..." He turned back to the others. "What do you think about the taxi?"

"Yeah, yeah! That'll be fun!"

When Jamie turned back he grinned at Becca.

"Tomorrow 10 p.m. Make sure you bring five hundred pounds. Or your mother will lose her taxi. And you might lose some teeth."

3 gaze – starrer Blick

Chapter 9

The passenger's seat was hot from the sun, Becca almost burnt her arms when she touched the backrest.

Her mother watched her from the side. "Do you really have to hang around with those boys?" She asked.

"Why don't you just start and leave if you don't like them?"

Becca rubbed her arms. They were still covered with goose pimples[1].

"I like that jacket," Georgina said from the back seat. Her distorted[2] index finger knocked against the window. "It looks like the ringmaster's[3] uniform."

"Hi Granny."

"Good afternoon, young lady. Are you satisfied with your seat? And have you told me your name?"

"The seat is perfect. I'm Becca, you know? Your granddaughter. I have the bedroom next to yours."

"Ah! You know you can lead a horse to water but you can't make it drink!"

"That is a very good one, thank you."

Becca was exhausted. And she didn't know what to do.

"So how was that test?" Her mother asked.

"It didn't take place. We had a problem. The school received a threatening letter. It turned out to be – harmless. But we didn't have proper lessons."

"That is unbelievable," her mother exclaimed. "Did they call the police?"

"I don't know," Becca said. From the bridge she could see that it was low tide. All the small fishing boats were lying on the wet ground on their sides – like dead fish.

1 goose pimples – Gänsehaut 2 distorted – verkrümmt 3 ringmaster – Zirkusdirektor

Exercise 32

Besserwisser: Was ist in den folgenden Sätzen richtig, Adjektiv (z.B. *light, good*) oder Adverb (z.B. *lightly, well*)? Setze die richtige Form ein.

1. *Jamie was (angry)* ________________.
2. *Jamie looked (angry)* ________________ *at Becca.*
3. *Becca behaved (frightful)* ________________.

Becca had to do something if she didn't want to end up the same way.

She cleared her throat and said: "Well, Mum? Could you lend[4] me some money?"

Leonora braked and looked at Becca.

"Again? What do you need all that money for? Clothes? By the way, where is your new leather jacket? I haven't seen it for days. Drugs?"

"Nonsense, drugs!! No." Becca hesitated. She would never be able to collect as much money as she needed by the following night. But she had to start somewhere. "I gave my jacket to Helen, she likes it so much. Just lent it. I – I need the money to go … to Glastonbury, to the festival. You know. With Helen. We have to buy our tickets in advance."

Her mother started the car again and pulled in between two other cars.

"If you want to have fun, you will have to earn money yourself, love. You know how hard I have to work to keep everything going. And, by the way, you are far too young to go to that kind of festival and stay overnight."

4 to lend – ausleihen

Exercise 33

Wortverdreher: Bilde Fragen aus den folgenden Sätzen, indem du die Wortstellung veränderst und – wo nötig – Wörter ergänzt.

1. *Ms Dingles suspected Becca of being a thief.*

   ____

2. *Dash wanted to get a proper job.*

   ____

3. *Jamie blackmailed Becca for money.*

   ____

I really know how hard you're working, Becca thought, and I'm sorry. "Oh come on. Dashiel Hunter is going too, he's grown up. How can I work and earn money while school is on? You always say I have to get my priorities right. School always comes first."

"The grass is always greener on the other side," Georgina threw in from the back.

"Dashiel Hunter? The famous gang Dashiel? Is he Helen's new boyfriend? Gosh[5]! Those wealthy girlies, always in search of the ultimate kick! But if you wanted to go, you could work during your holidays. Plenty of time. Go and apply for jobs in the old town, pasty and souvenir shops are always looking for help."

"But that's too late, I need the money now! The Glastonbury festival is before the holidays start. And the ticket office opens today. Tickets will soon be sold out."

5 gosh! – meine Güte!

"Well, you can go next year."

"But Helen is going this year. I can't leave her on her own. I told her I would come."

"You said this Dashiel would accompany her."

Becca groaned[6]. There was no way of telling her mother that Dash was her own boyfriend. Leonora would freak out. And on the other hand Becca was not sure herself if Dash was a good choice, if she could trust him. He had said he had left the gang. But he was still seeing them.

Exercise 34

Lückenfüller: Hänge das passende Frageanhängsel (*question tag*, z.B. *You haven't seen her, have you?*) an!

1. *You don't have to hang around with those guys, ________________?*
2. *You did take the wristwatch, ________________?*
3. *I can't come this afternoon, ________________?*

"But I want to go with Helen too. They are – Dashiel is just a friend. And I promised I would go."

"That wasn't very clever, was it?" Becca's mother said.

"Don't sell the skin before you have caught the bear[7]," Georgina said.

"Oh, thank you, Granny, that is very helpful," Becca replied.

"Can I feed the bears now?" the thin voice from the back seat said.

"No, Leonora, the carnivores[8] are too restless today. You have to be quiet now."

6 to groan – stöhnen 7 don't sell the skin before you have caught the bear – verkauf nicht das Fell, bevor du den Bären gefangen hast 8 carnivore – Raubtier

Her mother took Becca's hand and stroked it like a cat. "You can go next year, love. You know that Helen's family has a different – well – financial background. She could buy a leather jacket herself instead of taking yours ..."

"Oh Mum. That is so unfair."

Exercise 35

Gewusst, was: Verbinde die englischen Sprichwörter *(idioms)* mit der richtigen deutschen Übersetzung.

Don't cross your bridges before you come to them.	*Eigenlob stinkt.*
to take coals to Newcastle	*Kümmere dich nicht um ungelegte Eier.*
Don't toot your own horn.	*Eulen nach Athen tragen*

Becca felt tears running down her face. She turned away. She didn't want her mother to see her crying and misinterpret[9] everything. The bloody Glastonbury festival was the last thing Becca was interested in. She had to protect her mother's taxi. And her whole family.

And she had to find out about Dash. Who he really was and what he was after.

9 misinterpret – falsch deuten

Chapter 10

It was hot inside the conservatory[1], although all windows and the double glass doors were wide open.

Helen put her tablet PC on her lap and typed in:

10:30 at the beach kiosk. CU

She pressed the enter key[2]. It was high time to meet Bono172 in real life.

Helen kept the PC on her knees, just in case Bono172 should reply, and leaned back in her favourite[3] easy chair[4]. Becca had not yet called. What was wrong with her? What kind of secret did she share with the headmistress?

Helen liked this easy chair with its rose-covered fabric and the wooden ends of the armrests, carved[5] in the form of a lady's hands. This chair reminded her of a play her parents had taken her to last year at the Minack open air theatre. Something by Jane Austen. They had had furniture like this chair on stage. The theatre seats, unfortunately, were made of concrete. Her bottom had been sore after the play.

Helen checked her inbox. Although the lack of a message tone should have been clear enough. But you never knew. She needed something to brighten up her boring life.

After three weeks of daily chats she had finally agreed to meet Bono172. He had asked her so many times. And he was funny and intelligent and had exactly the degree of adventurousness[6] she needed right now.

Helen covered her eyes with her hands and looked towards the horizon. The lawn in front of the house looked like a putting

1 conservatory – Wintergarten 2 enter key – Eingabetaste 3 favourite – Llieblings- 4 easy chair – Sessel
5 to carve – schnitzen 6 adventurousness – Unternehmungslust

green. A palm tree at the far end of the garden marked the rim[7] where the cliff fell down to a tiny beach that only her family could reach via some crooked[8] old steps carved out of the rocks.

Exercise 36

Zeitreise: Setze die folgenden Verben ins Präsenz.

1. *Becca's mother (took) ________________ her hand and (stroked) ________________ it like a cat.*
2. *Helen (switched) ________________ her mobile on again.*
3. *Georgina (wanted) ________________ to go to the circus.*

The sun was still high up in the south-west. It threw a strong layer[9] of light over the smooth sea. The water looked like a mirror, reflecting the blue of the sky. A soft, warm wind came inside and caressed[10] Helen's face. She shivered despite the temperature.

Exercise 37

Wessen? Setze die folgenden Begriffe in den Genitiv.

1. *the young lady + backpack* ________________
2. *the harbour + entrance* ________________
3. *the mouse + hole* ________________

The door of her mother's greenhouse opened and Helen turned around as she came into the conservatory.

7 rim – Kante 8 crooked – krumm, schief 9 layer – dünne Schicht 10 to caress – liebkosen

"Hello darling," said her mother. "Have you seen my wristwatch?"

Helen automatically turned the tablet PC face down and smiled.

"Hi, Mummy. No, sorry."

"Hm, strange." Her mother shook her head and went on. "Finished your homework for today?"

"Yes, finished. I did a bit of revision[11] for the test they postponed today."

"Do you think your friend Becca has got anything to do with that threatening letter they got?"

Exercise 38

Satzsalat: Bringe die Wörter in die richtige Reihenfolge!

1. *was conservatory it hot the inside.*

   ____

2. *front of the in like a house looked putting the lawn green.*

   ____

3. *looked a mirror like the water.*

   ____

"No way, Mummy. How could you …?"

"Well, Helen, because you mentioned she was in the headmistress's office for quite a long time, and she didn't give you a chance to talk to her afterwards."

"But that could have been for many different reasons," Helen

11 to do revision – für eine Prüfung lernen

said. She noticed, too late, the doubtful tone of her voice.

"Such as...?"

Her mother pulled another easy chair closer and sat down close to Helen.

"She'll call me as soon as possible. Becca has a lot of obligations[12] at home, you see – the housework, her grandma, et cetera, et cetera."

Exercise 39

Vieles: Bilde den Plural der folgenden Substantive!

1. *tree* ________________
2. *bee* ________________
3. *advice* ________________

"I am not saying anything against Rebecca, believe me. She is a nice girl. She was very – helpful – with the planting and care of my orchids in the greenhouse last week, do you remember? And she can't be blamed for – well, for her parents splitting up. And for the whole taxi thing. What a strange situation! Who would want to earn her money driving people around?"

Not you, mother, Helen thought. That would be far too daring for such an ivory-tower[13] person as you.

Helen watched some sailing boats coming in for the night. Her mother had always refused to go on a sailing boat.

For me, Helen thought, driving a taxi would be exactly the right way to get among people, interesting people with a history and their own dreams for the future. Like Becca's friend Dash.

12 obligation – Verpflichtung 13 ivory-tower – Elfenbeinturm, weltfremd

Dash was – well. He was Becca's friend. But Helen would see Bono172. He was special too.

Her mother drove her hand through her hair. "And have you seen her leather jacket? She looks a bit like one of those Hell's Angels."

Exercise 40

Besserwisser: Steigere die folgenden Adjektive.

1. *friendly,* ________________, ________________
2. *wonderful,* ________________, ________________
3. *seldom,* ________________, ________________

"Oh Mummy!"

I wish I had a jacket like that, but my parents would never get me one. I'd get a designer leather jacket in a classic dark brown and in a boring style.

"Well, I'll see if Nora has made dinner." Helen's mother got up and went into the living room.

Chapter 11

Jack Jacobs leaned back from his desk and tried to relax. The pressure at school this morning had given him a bad stomach ache[1].

When he came home his landlady had been in the front garden cutting her roses. She had instantly realised how stressed out Jack was and led him into her living room. He had sat in her deceased husband's leather armchair and admired his collection of hunting paintings. The whole house reminded him of his parents. Who he missed a lot.

Meanwhile his landlady had prepared a cup of chamomile[2] tea and handed it over.

Jack's hands were trembling when he took the cup.

"Oh, you poor boy," the old lady said. "What happened? Did your exam ...?"

"No," Jack interrupted her. "There was a problem, a threatening letter arrived."

And he told her the whole story.

When he had finished, his landlady had patted his hand and shrugged her shoulders. Her light grey eyes rested on him like his grandmother's. She kept silent for some minutes. Finally she stood up and moved in front of the fireplace.

She patted her white hair, although every single hair was in place, and said: "Have you ever thought of – well. These kids today, they are different. So different from how we were."

Jack had nodded. "They are completely different from what I was like."

"Of course. It's not easy to be a teacher today, it must be much more difficult than it was when you were at school."

1 stomach ache – Magenschmerzen 2 chamomile – Kamille

"I know. It is a challenge. A challenge I wanted to meet when I started studying."

Exercise 41

Zeitreise: Setze die Verben in die einfache Vergangenheit (*past tense*, z. B. *went*)!

1. *The ferryman (wants) ________________ Dash as his employee.*
2. *Helen's mother (worries) ________________ about her daughter.*
3. *Becca's grandma (suffers) ________________ from Alzheimer's disease.*

The landlady watched him rubbing his knees. Jack could not keep his hands still. This subject made him feel so uncomfortable. He had not expected such a difficult situation at school, and this was his second try. The first school had sent him away as he had been unable to manage his class.

His parents didn't know about this – relocation[3], he called it, although it had actually been a dismissal[4].

The talk with his landlady had ended with her asking him if he had ever thought of doing something else for a living.

Jack turned over the next page of the new teaching unit he was trying to develop. It didn't work. It had never worked. He should have given up his studies the first time he had experienced a panic attack in front of a class. He was no teacher. He would never get used to either the lesson planning or the kids themselves.

3 relocation – Versetzung 4 dismissal – Entlassung

Exercise 42

Parallelwelten: Finde die Gegenteilpaare und verbinde sie mit Strichen.

smooth	*shallow*
deep	*expensive*
many	*rough*
weak	*few*
cheap	*strong*

He felt his cheek. It was a bit swollen and hot, as if something was wrong with his wisdom tooth[5]. That was the last thing he needed right now!

He picked up his mobile phone and looked at the display.

No new messages.

That was the only good thing to happen today.

5 wisdom tooth – Weisheitszahn

Chapter 12

After Becca had prepared the pizza for dinner, kneaded[1] the dough and put it aside to rise, chopped all the veggies and grated the cheese, she went to her room.

She had pretended to have too much homework to do to take care of Georgina. So her mother had taken Granny with her again in the taxi. Granny's farewell had been: "Nothing ventured, nothing gained[2]", and Becca had been thinking about this saying and her options since then.

At the moment she could see only two options.

And, unfortunately, Dash was not one of them. He pretended to be her friend, took her out for long walks and everything, but she had seen him hang around with his old gang. Exactly the same boy who had taken her leather jacket and who was blackmailing[3] her now.

Dash had talked a lot about how important it was to make the right decisions and to take responsibility for yourself. But how could Becca know whether he was telling her the truth or whether he was just playing with her? Could he be behind this threat? Laughing at her?

She felt sick. She had to find out first if she could trust him. Or not.

Becca switched on the computer and checked her e-mails. Nothing of interest. Dash didn't use a computer, he was outside all day long and sent her text messages or called her, like in the morning when she had been in Ms Dingles' office.

Becca closed the computer and lay down on her bed. She found her favourite cushion and snuggled down into it[4].

Dash was no option in the case.

1 to knead – kneten 2 nothing ventured, nothing gained – wer nicht wagt, der nicht gewinnt 3 to blackmail – erpressen 4 to snuggle down into/with sth. – mit etwas kuscheln

The first option was Helen, but Becca's stomach turned as she imagined how she would have to lie to get five hundred pounds from her.

Becca had to throw up[5]. She ran to the bathroom just in time to hit the toilet. She felt really poorly. But she had to do something or those guys would damage her mother's taxi. And maybe hurt her mother and her grandmother too. And herself. There was no escape.

EXERCISE 43

Lückenfüller: Setze die richtigen Präpositionen ein!

1. *Jack looked ________________ his mobile phone.*
2. *Helen was looking ________________ to meeting Bono172.*
3. *Becca had been thinking ________________ her options.*

Helen was Becca's best friend. Becca had betrayed[6] her once before. But she would have to do it again. Because Helen was the only person who might possibly be willing to give Becca that much money.

Becca threw cold water into her face and sneaked[7] back into her room. She sank onto her bed and picked up her mobile phone.

When she was about to dial Helen's number, the phone rang in her hand. She almost dropped it.

She put it to her ear, heard the voice and tried to swallow. But her throat was dry and her heart was racing. It was the last person she wanted to talk to right now: Dash.

5 to throw up – sich übergeben 6 to betray – betrügen, verraten 7 to sneak – schleichen

Chapter 13

"Becca, you are so … I don't know …" Dash followed a fishing boat with his eyes. The water was pulling out the boat and soon the riverbed[1] would be dry. He had known how the river looked at low tide since he was a young boy, all the boats lying on their sides like beached[2] whales. But today the image was stronger than ever before. Dash shivered. He felt a strange sense of loneliness which did not at all match the brilliant mood he had been in before he had called his girlfriend.

Dash tried again to convince Becca. "Come on, only one hour, just to celebrate a little bit!"

"I'm really sorry," Becca replied, "We'll have to cancel our date tonight altogether, I can't come."

Dash shook his head. Something was wrong, he felt, Becca did not react to his questions. She seemed like a shell, firmly closed. He had told her the good news about his job, wanted to celebrate this turning point together with her. But Becca had interrupted him instantly. He hadn't had a chance.

"Is there anything I can do for you?" Dash finally asked. But he knew the answer before Becca spoke.

"No, thanks. Everything is fine. I just have to take care of my Grandma. That's all. I'll call you tomorrow."

Dash sighed and pressed the red button on his mobile phone. He shrugged his shoulders.

Why was Becca behaving so strangely? Was she not happy for him about the job? They had talked about his wish to improve so often, and Becca had seemed so supportive.

Until now. Even if she had to take care of her grandma she could have shared his happiness. But she had not.

1 riverbed – Flussbett 2 beached – gestrandet

Exercise 44

Betrüger: Finde den Fehler in folgenden Sätzen.

1. *Becca threw cold water into her face and sneaked back into her room.*
2. *When she was after to dial Helen's number, the phone rang in her hand.*
3. *The water was pulling out the boat and soon the riverbed would be dry.*

What was wrong?

Was another man behind this?

No.

She would have told Dash.

Wouldn't she?

Yes. Dash could trust her.

Couldn't he?

Dash shrugged his shoulders.

Only a few weeks ago he would have called his mates and celebrated[3] with them. They would have gone to a pub for one beer. And would have come out again after many beers. In a mood they would have called good. And they would have kept on celebrating in the streets as they had done so many times before, drinking more alcohol, getting louder and more daring every minute. Looking out for what they thought were challenges. Like the fish boxes on the pier.

Dash wiped his eyes.

He knew for sure that none of his former mates would want to celebrate his new job with him.

3 to celebrate – feiern

Exercise 45

Besserwisser: Welche der folgenden Aussagen ist eindeutig richtig?

1. *Dash is living in Truro, where his aunt and uncle brought him up after his parents' death in a car accident.*
2. *Becca's father left the family some time ago. That is the reason for her mother driving a taxi.*
3. *Helen's parents are the owners of several hotels in Devon and Cornwall. They have lived in Looe for fifteen years.*

Chapter 14

Helen walked along the cliffs after lunch. She'd had to get out, could not stay with her mother all day and make small talk. She had to get some fresh air.

Bono172 had not yet texted back!

Some clouds had gathered over the horizon and Helen thought that a change of weather would fit her mood perfectly. A thunderstorm would be the perfect match. But that would spoil her plans to meet Bono172 later. And so she kept watching the clouds while she walked down the steps to the beach.

Her phone rang. It was Becca. Finally!

"I'm going to see this guy I told you about," Helen said. "Bono172. Tonight. Would you come with me? Just in case …" Helen left away any introduction and was surprised herself. What if Becca said yes and Bono172 didn't answer her text message?

"I would like to," Becca replied. "Really. But I can't. Mum is taking a passenger to a dinner in St. Ives and won't be back until late. I can't leave Grandma alone. I'm so sorry."

Helen stopped and sat down on a rock.

"Oh, sugar! Can't your mum take her with her in the taxi as always?"

"No, not at night. Grandma needs her sleep or she'll be ill tomorrow. So …"

"That's a real shame. But I'll go anyhow."

"Promise to be careful, will you?"

"I will, I will." Helen had difficulty hiding her disappointment[3]. She got up and followed the steps down the cliff. "Anyway, how are you?"

1 disappointment – Enttäuschung

Exercise 46

Buchstabensalat: Sortiere die Buchstaben so, dass sinnvolle Wörter entstehen!

1. *edrsortunthm* ____________________
2. *leatbrceion* ____________________
3. *apdispenomtint* ____________________

"I'm, well, I'm in real trouble ..."

"With Dingles, hm? Because of the letter?"

"Ah no, no way. That was ..." Becca paused. "That was because of a book I damaged. No big problem. No, I'm having trouble with my mother."

"Oh, come on, your mum is always so – supportive!"

"Not this time. It's because of my leather jacket. You know, the blue one. I've lost it and it was a birthday present from her. Expensive. I can't tell her I've lost it, she'd kill me ..."

Helen reached the beach. The clouds had gone, but she didn't feel any better.

Becca's excuse sounded somehow lame, unlike Becca, who had always been fond of adventures – like going out at night and seeing boys. Well, the part about seeing boys had stopped for Becca now, because of Dash. But the rest ...

"You're exaggerating[2]."

"No, I'm not. But I know the solution. I have to buy a new jacket. I've seen the same one in a shop in Truro, exactly the same. Five hundred pounds."

"Where the heck[3] are you going to get five hundred quid from?"

2 to exaggerate – übertreiben 3 where the hell/heck – wo zum Teufel

Exercise 47

Parallelwelten: Finde die Gegenteilpaare und verbinde sie mit Strichen.

active	*lend*
alike	*clear*
borrow	*lazy*
cloudy	*cowardice*
courage	*different*

Helen took a handful of sand and watched it disappear through her fingers. Everything was disappearing: her hope for a response from Bono172, Becca's reliability[4], her trust in Becca.

"I was hoping you could help me out, just until after the summer holidays. I'll find a job – I'll give you everything back in eight weeks' time?"

Oh Becca! Why are you lying to me?

Helen sat down on a rock. Again she looked at her mobile phone display. Nothing. Bono172 must be busy. Or had he lost interest in her since she had agreed to meet him?

"I haven't got that much money, Becca. I spend a lot on horse riding and golf lessons. To be honest, I've only got fifty left. That's all for this month. And I'll need that to pay the bill for my mobile phone. I'm sorry."

Helen heard Becca sigh at the other end of the line. She seemed to have real problems if she needed that much money.

"What about Dash? Can't he help you out?"

"Dash. He called today to tell me that he has got a job now.

4 reliability – Glaubwürdigkeit

At the harbour. But he hasn't been paid yet. And I – oh, forget it. Good luck for tonight. I want to hear everything about Bono172 tomorrow."

"Okay, bye."

Well, even now that Becca wasn't going to join her, Helen had to escape her parents' closeness and never-ending concern about her well-being. She was almost sixteen and far from being a child who needed full-time helicopter parents hovering over her!

A "pling" indicated that she had a new message.

CU 10:30 tonight!

Bingo!

Exercise 48

Zeitreise: Setze die Verben ins Perfekt (*present perfect*, z.B. *has gone*)!

1. *By midday Jack (goes) ________________ home.*
2. *When her father comes home, Helen (leaves) ________________ the conservatory.*
3. *When Leonora calls home, Becca (prepares) ________________ the pizza dough.*

It was not easy to find a good example of the male species in this corner of Cornwall! Most of the locals were old, unemployed or going out with somebody else – like Dashiel.

He belonged to Becca. Who had turned out to be a traitor[5], as she had lied to Helen about her jacket. Helen wiped her eyes.

5 traitor – Verräter

That wind!

Or, at least, Becca had secrets.

Helen had seen one of the gang wearing Becca's leather jacket only yesterday.

What was going on between him and Becca?

Chapter 15

Becca jumped down from the garage onto the dustbin[1].

Oh flip[2]!

She waited until the rattling noise from the dustbin lid stopped. It was too loud! Her mother's bedroom window was at the back of the house. But Georgina's window looked over the garage, like her own. And it was open.

Becca held her breath and listened carefully.

"Out of the frying pan into the fire[3]," came Granny's sleepy voice.

Becca clenched her teeth[4]. Granny was right. After another minute she was sure that her mother was fast asleep and hadn't heard the noise. She always got up early, in case any tourists needed an early lift to Penzance to take the ferry to the Scilly Isles.

Becca rushed on. Her mother's taxi was parked in front of their house right by the sea as usual. Becca chose to walk on that side of the road, as most people used the other side. She didn't want to be recognised.

After the phone call with Helen some hours ago, Becca had decided to take option two:

Wait till it gets dark. Climb out of the window. Break into the school building and Ms Dingles' office. Steal the watch. Pawn it the next day. Becca had searched the internet for a pawnshop[5] nearby[6]. There was one in Truro. She could get there the following morning on the 11:15 bus, skipping school, and would be back by 6 p.m. Early enough to meet the gang and deliver the protection money[7] at 10 p.m.

She intended[8] to keep the rest. As the headmistress had said, the watch was worth several thousand.

1 dustbin – Mülltonne 2 flip (coll.) – Mist, verdammt! 3 out of the frying pan into the fire – vom Regen in die Traufe 4 to clench one's teeth – die Zähne zusammenbeißen 5 pawnshop – Pfandhaus 6 nearby – nahe gelegen 7 protection money – Schutzgeld 8 to intend to – vorhaben, etwas zu tun

Becca was determined not to spend the money otherwise, to go to Glastonbury, for example. She would save it, apply for a job at the supermarket; hopefully she would get one over the summer holidays. And pay every single penny back to the pawnbroker[9]. By the end of the holidays she would be out of this mess and able to give the watch back to its owner. And nothing serious would have happened.

Becca rounded a corner and kept out of the pools of light the streetlights were throwing on the pavement. There were only some tourists on their way back from the pubs, laughing and chatting away. They didn't look at her, were too busy having fun. Which was good.

Becca crossed the Looe bridge and looked around. She moved quickly to get out of sight. There was no protection on the bridge. But after that the woods would start and give her shelter. Becca turned left after crossing the bridge. The touristy part of Looe was to the right. All of a sudden she was alone.

Exercise 49

Betrüger: Finde die falsche Übersetzung des Sprichwortes.

not be able to hold a candle to someone	*jemandem das Wasser nicht reichen können*
to handle someone with kid gloves	*jemanden wie ein rohes Ei behandeln*
Haste makes waste.	*Eile mit Weile.*
That's not your cup of tea.	*Das ist nicht deine Teetasse.*
Once bitten, twice shy.	*Gebranntes Kind scheut das Feuer.*

9 pawnbroker – Pfandleiher

Becca hurried on until she reached the school entrance. She went through it and round to the back of the building.

She had to climb over a fence to reach the gym. She wanted to get in there, but all the windows were closed. If she smashed one of them it would make a lot of noise. She looked around for another opportunity.

There!

One of the classroom windows on the ground floor was open a small slit. Becca tried to push it open, but it didn't work. Her arm muscles were aching with the strain[10]. And her fingers were trembling[11]. She couldn't hang around here for ages!

Somebody might see her.

In the back of her mind she heard her grandma's voice: "Nothing ventured, nothing gained."

She took one of the decorative stones surrounding the playing field, smashed the window and crawled in quickly.

10 strain – große Anstrengung 11 to tremble – zittern

Chapter 16

Dash clenched his fists inside his cargo jeans and counted backwards from 100 to 90. His jaw muscles[1] relaxed a bit. At least enough for him to speak.

"What are you trying to tell me, Jamie Dagger? That my girlfriend gave her leather jacket to you? As a present?"

Jamie strutted from one side to the other, a heavy turkey trying to impress the other displaying[2] mate. He had had a lot of beer at the pub they had just left, while Dash had kept to two beers only and some water. Which had made the others laugh and take the mickey out of him[3].

"What do you think?" Jamie replied and turned back to his pals[4]. As if addressing them with his rhetorical question.

The five guys chuckled[5] or grinned stupidly. Their lack of willingness to think for themselves had always repelled[6] Dash.

"Becca would never give her jacket away, she loves it too much. It was a present from her mother, and she knows how hard she had to work for it." Dash controlled the volume of his voice. And his anger.

"Who said she didn't love me? It was a kind of love token." Jamie was still strutting around, but now he looked like a fighter in the boxing ring.

Some tourists came out of the pub and stopped.

"Everything okay, guys?" a man asked into Dash's direction.

"Everything's fine, yeah! Goodnight."

The man nodded and followed the others who had waited a little way further down the narrow lane.

Dash's toes prickled and his arm muscles tightened. He wanted to move, to hit this liar in the face. But that would not

1 jaw muscle – Kiefermuskel 2 to display – hier: balzen 3 to take the mickey out of s.o. (coll.) – sich über jmd. lustig machen 4 pal (coll.) – Kumpel 5 to chuckle – leise lachen 6 to repel – abstoßen

solve any problems. It was better to stay calm. Jamie alone would be a challenge Dash would possibly be able to tackle, but six against one were too much.

Exercise 50

Fundstücke: Finde im Anfang des Kapitels die englischen Entsprechungen zu diesen Sätzen und unterstreiche sie.

1. *Seine Wangenmuskeln entspannten sich etwas. Wenigstens so weit, dass er sprechen konnte.*
2. *Das hatte die anderen zum Lachen gebracht und sie versuchten, ihn zu veräppeln.*
3. *Ihr Mangel an Bereitschaft, selbst zu denken, hatte Dash immer schon abgestoßen.*

Dash looked up. A seagull was flying across the lane, crying. Some of its droppings[7] landed on Jamie's head and some more on the chests and shoulders of some of his mates. Dash had to laugh out loud.

The bird had appeared at the right moment. Dash decided it was a friend, who had given a very vivid[8] example of what to do with these boys.

"Make sure no droppings are left on Becca's jacket. She wouldn't like that!"

Dash turned and left his former gang standing with their mouths open.

7 droppings – Kot 8 vivid – lebhaft

Chapter 17

Helen was happy. Her parent's had left the house at 6 p.m. to watch a play at the Jamaica Inn, a place near Bodmin her father fancied for a reason Helen could not understand.

The pub was a place the famous author Daphne du Maurier had chosen for one of her novels. But that was ages ago, and today the place was nothing more than a run-down tourist trap[1], a hotel with a self-service bar which offered only fast food of a lower quality than all the burger bars Helen had ever visited. A tiny little museum of Daphne du Maurier memorabilia[2] was part of the attraction, and that was where the local Daphne du Maurier group, an amateur dramatics society[3], used to perform their plays every year in summer.

Her parents liked to go there every time, but after several attempts they had accepted last summer that Helen did not want to join them. Which was a lucky coincidence tonight, as it saved her from lying and pretending to go to bed. And from climbing out of the window like a burglar[4] on the retreat[5].

Helen had left the house through the front door and walked down Hannafore Lane. It was dark now, and the street was calm and almost deserted[6].

She was in a brilliant mood. She had dressed as cool as possible, with tight black jeans and a crop top[7] she had bought secretly for a special occasion. Today was this occasion, she had never worn the top before.

When Helen approached the Looe bridge on her way to meet Bono172, she suddenly stopped. Right across the street the headmistress, Ms Dingles, came walking down the hill down Polperro Road, where her house was. What was she

1 tourist trap – Touristenfalle 2 memorabilia – Erinnerungsstücke 3 amateur dramatics society – Laienschauspieltruppe 4 burglar – Einbrecher 5 retreat – Rückzug 6 deserted – verlassen 7 crop top – bauchfreies Top

doing out that late? She lived alone. Was she on her way to meet a man?

Exercise 51

Lückenfüller: Hänge das passende Frageanhängsel (*question tag*, z.B. *You haven't seen her, have you?*) an!

1. *Jamie Dagger was wearing Becca's jacket, ________________?*
2. *Dash had always been repelled by Jamie's stupidity, ________________?*
3. *Helen didn't go with her parents to the play, ________________?*

Helen waited for a moment until the head had passed Helen's hiding place in a house doorway. Fortunately some tourists were just leaving the amusement arcade[8] by the bridge. They were obviously on their way to Fore Street, the main street leading into the old town. Helen could follow Ms Dingles quite easily, as she was concentrating on talking to somebody on her mobile phone. She didn't look left or right.

Helen managed to get closer to her headmistress behind one huge tourist. She leaned forward, straining to hear what Ms Dingles was saying. When the people in front of her stopped talking for a moment, Helen could hear every word Ms Dingles said to her listener.

8 amusement arcade – Spielhalle

Chapter 18

Sandra Dingles had not yet come to terms[1] with the threatening letter affair. She had been thinking about it all evening. She still was not sure whether she should have called the police. And she could not make up her mind on how to handle the watch affair. Should she have insisted on taking Rebecca home and talking to her grandmother? The story Rebecca had told her about finding the watch in the street was quite unbelievable. But what reason could Rebecca have to lie? And to steal, in the worst case?

But the cherry on the cake[2] had been Jayjay's – she definitely had to stop calling him the nickname the kids had given him, that was too embarrassing, she should be ashamed of herself! Well, Jacobs' corrections of Philippa Shneider's test had been a total shambles[3]! He had corrected correct words and grammar! Had he lost his mind altogether[4]?

She carefully locked the front door and hurried down the road to the village centre. After hours of fruitless pondering she had decided to ask her sister's advice. Her sister Ruth was waiting at her house for a very late bite[5]. This was an emergency and the only reason why Ruth had finally agreed on seeing her sister that late.

Ruth was a former human resources[6] manager who used to work for a global player[7] with its headquarters in London. She had moved here after retiring[8], as had many others. She knew everything about how to lead people – or how to fire[9] them.

Rushing down to the bridge it came into Sandra's mind that Ruth always insisted on evidence[10]. But she had left Philippa's test with Jayjay's corrections at school. She had to get it! Sandra took her mobile out of her handbag and dialled.

1 to come to terms with sth. – sich mit etwas abfinden 2 the cherry on the cake – das Sahnehäubchen 3 shambles – heilloses Durcheinander 4 altogether – gänzlich 5 late bite – später Happen 6 human resources – Personalabteilung 7 global player – internationaler Konzern 8 to retire – in Rente gehen 9 to fire – kündigen 10 evidence – Beweis

Exercise 52

Just do it: Unterstreiche die Verben im vorigen Absatz und konjugiere sie durch.

"I'll be late I'm afraid, pet[11]. Sorry, but I've left something at school. A masterpiece of correcting, I can tell you, performed by our esteemed Jayjay Jacobs. I really need your advice on how to sort this out[12] …"

11 pet – Liebling 12 to sort sth. out – etwas loswerden

Chapter 19

"Excuse me???"

The fat man in front of Helen turned his head and looked into her face, which was almost touching his shoulder.

"Sorry," Helen murmured and put some space between herself and the man.

Ms Dingles had said "pet"! So there must be a man in her life! That was interesting!

Unfortunately Helen didn't have time to follow her up the hill to find out who "pet" was. She watched Ms Dingles turn left.

Helen overtook the tourists to get them between herself and the headmistress just in case she would turn around.

The tourists followed Helen through the narrow paved Fore Street leading into the old town. But at the end of the main street they entered one of the pubs.

And Helen was on her own, heading towards the beach at the far end of the village. In front of one of the pubs she saw a group of teenagers lingering about[1]. They were quite noisy. Helen took a right turn to the East Looe River. She didn't want to meet the local gang or drunken tourist teenagers.

It was quiet at the harbour – apart from some seagulls crying. Most locals were usually at home this time of night, and the tourists were vanishing one after the other.

Helen could hear the tide coming in, washing the walls of the quay on her right.

"Hi Helen, you're out late. All on your own?"

Helen's heart stopped beating and a layer of goose pimples ran down her back. But when the man stepped into the light of

1 to linger about – herumhängen

the old street lamp she recognised Dashiel. He came strolling[2] out of a narrow lane.

His eyes were as dark as his hair, and a thin shadow of a three-day beard covered his chin. He looked like a Spanish pirate. Who her parents would despise[3]. But for Helen it was more than acceptable.

"Hi Dash. I will not be on my own for long. I'm on my way to …" she stopped. Why, for God's sake, didn't she want to tell him about Bono172?

"And yourself? Without Becca tonight?"

"Ahem. She cancelled our date because of her grandmother. Which she's never done before."

Helen nodded. "She's acting a bit …" she searched for a word which wouldn't sound too negative.

"Strange?" Dash said with a big question mark at the end of his remark.

Exercise 53

Können und dürfen: Übersetze die folgenden Sätze und verwende *to be able to* oder *to be allowed to*.

1. *Kann Helen nachts alleine ausgehen?*

   ____

2. *Kann Ms Dingles den Junglehrer Jack einfach entlassen?*

   ____

3. *Kann Becca das Fenster mit einem Stein einwerfen?*

   ____

2 to stroll – schlendern 3 to despise – geringschätzen, ablehnen

"Strange, confused? I don't know what she's doing. It seems as if she keeps out of my way[4] most of the time."

"I thought she was only like that towards me," Dash said in a softer voice.

He looks sad, somehow, Helen thought.

"No," she replied. "Becca really has changed over the last few days. Something must have happened, but she doesn't want to talk."

"Hmm, so you don't know if there is …"

Dash looked down and paused. Did he suspect the same as Helen?

When the pause stretched as far as the bird island across the bay, Helen looked at her watch and cleared her throat.

"Well, I'll have to hurry up. Almost ten."

"And who are you meeting tonight? Somebody I know?"

"Somebody I don't even know in real life," Helen said with a rough laugh.

"You're kidding[5]! You're not seeing one of those internet paedophiles, are you?"

Dash grabbed Helen's elbow and turned her towards himself until she had to look into his eyes.

"Definitely not!" Helen shrieked. Her voice was too high-pitched[6], she heard it herself.

"I've known him for weeks. We just haven't met till now. I have to hurry, I don't want to keep him waiting."

She shook off Dashiel's hand, smiled to take the harshness[7] from her words and waved at him.

"Take care[8]!" she heard him say in a deep voice.

4 to keep out of s.o.'s way – jmd. aus dem Weg gehen 5 to kid – veräppeln, scherzen 6 high-pitched – schrill 7 harshness – Härte 8 take care – machs gut, pass auf dich auf

Chapter 20

He would never be able to finish this teaching unit[1]!

Jack closed his mobile phone and put it into his jeans pocket. He stood up from his desk and walked round and round his small room on the first floor. He felt trapped, needed more space!

His mother had tried to encourage him again, had told him how hard the start at school had been for herself, but he was not like her! Nor was he like his father, who was a big shot at a private bank in London.

Jack remembered the headmistress calling him into her office the day before. She had wanted to see his corrections on a test. And had not given it back to him this morning. What could that mean?

Jack stopped and sat down on his bed.

What if the headmistress disagreed with his corrections?

What if she dismissed him like the other school?

What would his parents say if he told them he wanted to change his – well, career sounded a bit over the top. What about "line of business[2]"?

That sounded professional.

But was teaching a "line of business"? Would his father agree on this definition? Or would he call Jack a loser right to his face?

Jack jumped up and started walking again.

If he could only prove he was on the right track, was able to fulfill his parents' high expectations. If he could only show them at least a girlfriend! To prove he was normal!

Jack rubbed his cheek. The tooth was hurting now, he felt the blood pulsating under his skin. It was painful.

1 teaching unit – Unterrichtseinheit 2 line of business – Branche

Exercise 54

Was wäre, wenn: Ergänze die fehlenden Verbformen in den folgenden If-Sätzen (Typ 1).

1. *If Becca acts strangely towards Dash, he (withdraw) ________________ from her.*
2. *If Helen meets Bono172, her parents (be) ________________ really annoyed.*
3. *If Dash convinces Helen not to go, Bono172 (not achieve) ________________ his aim.*

He sat down at his desk and took the old-fashioned fountain pen[3] in both hands. He could hear his mother's voice: "This is the old Mont Blanc pen my father gave me when he retired from being dean[4] at Cambridge. He gave it to me as an encouragement to eliminate all mistakes from my students' literary attempts with red ink." She had handed Jack the fountain pen together with a glass jar full of red ink and added: "Don't let the red ink dry out. Don't be shy now. Mistakes are not bad, so long as you find them and teach others to avoid them. That is your task. In your job as a teacher. And in life." His mother had closed his finger around the pen and patted his fist. "You will make a perfect teacher!"

Jack turned the pen between his fingers. He hated this bloody[5] symbol of his uselessness, of his incapability[6] to teach. He was incapable of eliminating his own mistakes. How should he correct others?

He clenched his teeth and felt the pain of the inflamed tooth at the back. And at the moment when the pain shot into his tooth, the fountain pen broke in two.

3 fountain pen – Füllfederhalter 4 dean – Dekan 5 bloody (coll.) – scheiß… (ugs.) 6 incapability – Unfähigkeit

Exercise 55

Nicht dürfen: Übersetze die folgenden Sätze.

1. *Becca darf nicht in die Schule einbrechen.*

   ____

2. *Lehrer dürfen nicht unfair sein.*

   ____

3. *Georgina darf nicht alleine bleiben.*

   ____

Red ink spread on the desk, like blood. As if something was dying.

Jack looked at his wristwatch.

He would not be able to get to sleep. He would have to get out into the fresh air, to get rid of this feeling of being trapped[7].

Jack took his coat and left the house.

7 trapped – gefangen

Chapter 21

"Oh sugar," Becca hissed[1].

Her left knee was bleeding from a shard[2] of broken glass she had kneeled[3] on climbing inside the school building. Now there was a big tear[4] in her jeans.

She brushed off the little pieces of glass from her legs and hurried to the classroom door.

Becca breathed in deeply and held her breath[5]. She carefully turned the door knob. And smiled. It was her lucky night. The door was not locked.

Becca hurried down the corridor without switching the neon lights on. She didn't need to. The classroom doors contained panes of glass and let in some light from the streetlamps. The headmistress's office was beyond the secretary's. Both doors were unlocked. Becca chuckled[6].

They should be more careful if they want to keep burglars away!

She closed the door behind her and sat down on Ms Dingles' chair behind her desk.

The room was dark and Becca noticed[7] a vague smell of something chemical, maybe the polish for the old-fashioned desk with its carvings.

The watch will be in the desk, Becca thought, as she couldn't see a safe or any other safe storage for confidential files – or for jewellery. She turned the beam of her torch[8] onto the desk.

She pulled the drawers out, three on each side, one after the other, examined the content. There were tests in one, all kinds of granola bars[9] in the second, organising stuff like scissors, stapler[10],

1 to hiss – zischen 2 shard – Scherbe 3 to kneel – knien 4 tear – Riss 5 to hold one's breath – die Luft anhalten 6 to chuckle – leise lachen 7 to notice – wahrnehmen 8 torch – Taschenlampe 9 granola bar – Müsliriegel 10 stapler – Hefter

tape and paper in the third. On the other side the three drawers turned out to be one door. Behind it Becca found nothing but a half-empty bottle of French – what was it? Becca took the bottle to read the label – French Cognac, with six glasses. Amazing[11]! Did Ms Dingles drink?

Exercise 56

Verbbeuger: Ergänze die fehlenden Konjunktionsformen der folgenden Verben (z. B. *go, went, gone*)!

1. ________________, *bound,* ________________
2. ________________, ________________, *blown*
3. ________________, *drank,* ________________

Okay, Becca thought, the watch has to be in the only drawer with a lock, right in the middle under the table top[12].

Her fingers trembled and she had to swallow several times. She felt for the screwdriver in the back pocket of her trousers. She was well prepared. Then she breathed in and out again and pulled the drawer. It was not locked! It opened without any resistance!

Becca's heart jumped. She pulled the drawer out as far as possible and stood up to get a better view of what it contained. A lot of stuff was lying in front of her: pencils, which looked really posh[13], a small container, too small for a wristwatch. Becca pushed it aside. There were toffees and a lipstick, more scissors and a laser pointer, a bunch of keys[14]. But no wristwatch!

Becca felt a strange shiver run down her spine[15]. It had to be

11 amazing – erstaunlich, verblüffend 12 table top – Tischplatte 13 posh – todschick, nobel 14 bunch of keys – Schlüsselbund 15 spine – Wirbelsäule

here! Her heart stopped beating and started again, far too quickly, when she started to forage[16] in the drawer again.

And then she heard something else.

A familiar voice shouting: "Hello?"

16 to forage – herumkramen

Chapter 22

Dash waited until Helen had vanished around the next corner, then he followed her.

He felt concerned. Not only about Becca, who apparently had some serious problems, not only with him.

Why doesn't she tell me what's wrong? Dash thought. I could help her. Well, at least I would do my best, no matter what kind of trouble she's in. Only this story about Jamie and her jacket … The boy is just a poor pitiable[1] idiot who bullies others to make them feel even worse than himself. And he doesn't even realise that it won't help him a bit.

It had taken quite a long time for Dash to learn that. But since he had met Becca he had been impressed at how she and her mother had managed to cope with the loss of her father and with her grandmother's Alzheimer's. That must have been a huge emotional effort and, moreover, it had changed everything in their lives. But they had managed, although the situation was not ideal. And so would he. Because he had the capacity and the energy and the strength to change his situation.

Meanwhile he had reached the open place by the beach. The full moon was hanging over the scenery like a Chinese lantern, all the clouds were gone.

Dash stopped in the shadow of the lane and watched Helen sit down on one of the iron benches, her back turned to him and to the nearby kiosk.

Helen must be totally nuts, Dash thought. Why was she taking such a risk, meeting somebody she didn't know? And although she had not admitted that she knew the guy from the internet, Dash knew from Becca that Helen was on the PC and on social

1 pitiable – bemitleidenswert

networks all day long.

Helen looked at her watch again – it must be the seventh time.

Dash kept in the shadow of a souvenir shop entrance, as close to Helen as possible, but hidden from the eyes of anybody approaching Helen's position.

Now she brushed her fingers through her blonde hair. She seemed nervous. And, as far as Dash could judge her situation, she was absolutely right to be.

Dash bent forward to get a glimpse[2] of the surroundings. Nobody there.

When he had met Helen for the first time he had been impressed[3] at how "normal" Becca's best friend was. He had expected a spoiled[4] girl, from what Becca had told him about Helen's parents and house and everything. There was only a very small group of wealthy people living in Looe. And none of them were locals[5]. Like Helen's family they had come as tourists and moved here – if their profession and wealth[6] allowed – because of the "outstanding natural beauty" of the place, as the Looe tourist website boasted[7]. Only a few locals had reached such a high standard of living. But not through bullying others – like Jamie and his gang – but through hard work and a lot of determination[8] and energy, like some of the local hotel and restaurant owners. And that was exactly what Dash would do: learn as much as possible, work hard and make a fortune in the end.

Helen looked at her watch again. She could not see what Dash saw: a man who was sneaking closer from behind the kiosk!

Dash hesitated. Did that boy really mean a threat for Helen? Or was he just a decent guy? In that case Dash would leave instantly. He was no peeping Tom[9]!

But why did that man sneak? And why was he wearing a coat in summer? And a strange hat?

2 glimpse – flüchtiger Blick 3 to be impressed – beeindruckt sein 4 spoiled – verwöhnt 5 locals – Einheimische 6 wealth – Vermögen 7 to boast – angeben 8 determination – Entschlossenheit 9 peeping Tom (coll.) – Spanner

Now the man – he was really tall and had broad shoulders – reached Helen's bench and stepped in front of her. Helen looked up.

Were they talking?

Dash couldn't see what the man did, nor understand a word if they were talking. But Helen got up as if she had rheumatism or had been asleep.

Something was totally wrong.

Exercise 57

Besserwisser: Welche der folgenden Aussagen ist falsch?

1. *Ms Dingles went to school at night to pick up the test Jack Jacobs had corrected.*
2. *Becca had sent Georgina on a trip with Leonora when she climbed out of the window.*
3. *Dash followed Helen to protect her from a man with bad intentions.*

Chapter 23

"Hello?"

Something was strange, Sandra could feel it with every nerve in her shoulders and in her neck.

She switched on the light and hurried towards the secretary's office. All the classroom doors were closed, no lights were on, but the office door stood wide open, which was unusual. She would have to give out new instructions about closing doors at the end of the working day. That was another point on her agenda: get a new master key system[1] for the whole building. The board of governors[2] would not be amused! Since Jayjay – oh no, she had done it again! – since that young man had broken her key the whole system had been damaged and nobody could lock the doors.

Sandra grabbed her own bunch of keys firmly and entered her office. There was a strange noise inside. Had she left her computer switched on?

A dark figure was in her office! Sandra switched on the light, but she was too far away to stop the intruder[3]. By the time she turned round he had quickly jumped out of the window. Sandra stepped to the window and leaned out as far as possible without falling out.

"Hey you! Stop!"

Exercise 58

Hauptsache: Unterstreiche die Substantive (keine Namen!) im vorigen Absatz und setze sie in den Plural oder Singular.

1 master key system – Schließsystem 2 board of governors – Aufsicht führende Schulbehörde 3 intruder – Eindringling

But the dark figure had vanished behind the trees that bordered[4] the street.

Judged by its stature it could have been a young boy or a girl. Or a thin grown-up of her own size. One of her students?

Sandra closed the window, it was not damaged, and turned to her desk. What had the intruder been after?

The computer was still there, and the cupboard where the safe was hidden was closed. Good, very good.

Even her desk was in perfect order.

Sandra opened the drawers, one after the other. Everything seemed to be okay. Only the monitor of her PC stood in a slightly changed position, she thought. She must have interrupted a burglar who wanted to steal the technical equipment!

Sandra opened the desk door and poured[5] herself a large Cognac.

This'll be something to tell Ruth!

4 to border – säumen 5 to pour – eingießen

Chapter 24

Becca ran down the hill without looking back. She did not pay attention to the streetlights or passing cars. She only wanted to get a safe distance from school.

What the hell was Ms Dingles doing there that late? But who cares anyhow? I'm done for[1], no watch, no money.

Becca slowed down when her throat started to hurt from the dryness. She had reached the small church with the stony steps overgrown[2] with white blossoms, by the road leading uphill to Western Looe, and sank down on the steps. The perfect place to recover from a burglary – and to prepare for the final fight with the gang!

Pray! Becca thought, if I only could believe in God and pray! He might help!

She got up and stumbled down the street. Her cut knee was still hurting, but who cared? Tomorrow night her mother would lose her taxi and nobody knew what Becca would lose if she tried to protect the car.

Becca rounded the next corner and the wide sea opened in front of her with a full moon above. Everything was bathed in a ghostly blue light and Becca shivered. She walked on and pondered her options.

Give up? But that wouldn't change a thing. The gang will not accept that I don't have the money.

Talk to Mum? Never, she would call the police and everything would get even worse.

Dash? That would be the best solution. If I could only trust him. But he is still hanging around with those guys. And his situation hasn't changed much since he announced he was looking

1 done for – erledigt 2 overgrown – überwuchert

for work. Ferryman! He would soon be back with his old mates. If he ever really left the gang. No, I can't trust him.

Exercise 59

Lückenfüller: Ergänze das fehlende Wort!

1. *Ms Dingles would have to give out new instructions about ________________ doors.*
2. *The headmistress opened the desk door and ________________ herself a large Cognac.*
3. *Dash couldn't see what the guy was doing, nor could he ________________ a word.*

Becca walked past the big hotel and felt a strange sense of irritation.

What is wrong? Apart from everything about me? Something to do with the moonlight … It seems to be pulsating.

She felt the tension creep[3] up her arms, and when her mother's house came into sight a light was flashing, blinding Becca again and again. She started to run.

Has the gang already taken action? And has Mum called the police?

Becca reached her home. But it was not the police. It was an ambulance. Two men in orange uniforms were carrying a stretcher[4].

Becca's throat cramped, she could hardly breathe.

"Granny!" she shouted.

Her Granny was lying on the stretcher, Becca's mother at her side, holding her hand.

3 to creep – kriechen 4 stretcher – Trage

"What – what's happened?" Becca said when she reached the ambulance car.

"They say it was a stroke[5]," her mother replied. The yellow light from their hall was on her face. It was grey.

Becca looked into her Granny's eyes. They looked puzzled, disorientated and fearful. Her skin was white and one corner of her mouth was hanging down a bit.

When she focused on Becca one corner of her mouth lifted a bit into a tiny smile. She tried to say something, moved her lips, but only a strange murmur and fragments of words came out.

"Wait," Becca said to the carriers. "Please!"

"We can't wait, time is the most important factor in saving her," the man at the end of the stretcher said to Becca.

Her mother looked at her with a sadness in her eyes Becca had never seen before, not even when her father had left.

"Go inside, dear, go to bed and try to get some sleep," her mother said in a low voice. "I'll go to hospital with Granny."

"Can't I come too?" Becca asked.

Exercise 60

Strippenzieher: Verbinde die folgenden *phrasal verbs* (Verb mit Partikel) mit der richtigen deutschen Übersetzung.

keep away	*aufpassen*
keep up	*verschieben*
look out	*suchen*
look for	*(sich) fernhalten*
put off	*weitermachen*

5 stroke – Schlaganfall

"No, I don't know how long this will take. You have to get up early for school. Take care."

The paramedics[6] gently pushed the stretcher into the ambulance and Becca's mother followed.

When they were about to close the door Georgina moved a bit and murmured something. To Becca it sounded like "Don't cross your bridges before you come to them[7]".

"Thank you, Granny, and – take care!"

Becca stood for a while on the pavement in front of their house and looked after the ambulance, even when it had long vanished.

"I have already crossed my bridges," Becca whispered. "And you too, Granny!"

Becca felt as if she would never be able to move again, as if her body and soul were frozen.

6 paramedics – Sanitäter 7 don't cross your bridges before you come to them – sorge dich nicht, bevor du Anlass dazu hast

Chapter 25

Dash couldn't see the man's face, the hat threw a shadow over it. But Helen looked troubled[1], she turned away.

All of a sudden the guy stepped back so Helen had a view of his whole body and he made a strange noise. He moved his hand quickly in front of him and opened his coat.

Helen started whimpering[2] like a kitten, Dash could hardly hear it, nobody else would hear her.

"Holy cow!" Dash hissed.

He could not see a thing apart from bare[3] skin, but Helen would have seen all the details.

Dash did not think. He sprang forward and was at Helen's side in only a few steps. He shouted "fire, fire," but there was nobody around to help. And in fact Dash didn't need help.

The man stood frozen as an iceberg. Dash still could not see his face. But the rest of his front body was clearly to be seen. Out of the corner of his eye Dash realised that Helen had turned away and covered her face with both hands.

Dash did not hesitate nor think. It was his body acting, not his brain. But deep down in his heart he felt it was right to use his physical strength now. He put all his energy into the one stroke and hit the man with his fist right into his face. The other hand slammed[4] instinctively into the guy's stomach.

The man made a sound like an empty barrel falling on the floor, tilted forward and held his belly. He would be on his knees the next second.

Dash rubbed his knuckles[5] and breathed in deeply as he had done many time before when he had been a member of the gang. He turned around and looked how Helen was doing.

1 troubled – aufgewühlt, beunruhigt 2 to whimper – wimmern 3 bare – nackt, entblößt 4 to slam – kräftig zuschlagen 5 knuckle – Fingerknöchel

She was in tears, still covering her face.

"I'm such an idiot," she murmured.

Dash didn't know how to comfort her without putting his arms around her. He pushed his hands into his pockets.

And when he turned back to the man a second later, he had vanished[6].

6 to vanish – verschwinden

Chapter 26

Becca left the hospital the next day at 2 p.m.

Leonora had stayed there and called the school early to tell them that Becca wouldn't come because she had to support her mother and grandmother by bringing clothes and toiletries[1]. Which Becca had taken there in the morning.

Georgina's situation was serious. They had been waiting for a doctor to tell them the details all morning. Becca had been happy after her mother's phone call to the school secretary. It seemed that Ms Dingles had not recognised Becca the night before. That was good news. Becca didn't want to contribute to the sad situation at the moment.

Over the last few hours she had realised that her burglary was the least of her problems compared to what would happen the next night. She had had time enough to figure out that she was lost. And Leonora and the taxi too.

Becca felt sick, she had to swallow away the sour taste on the back of her tongue again and again in order not to throw up. But it came back within minutes. Her stomach was aching and she had a bad headache. Her back felt stiff. Half an hour ago her mother had chucked Becca out[2] of the hospital.

"You're making me nervous, dear. If you can't sit still, go home and prepare everything for Granny's return. Bed and towels. Put some on the mattress[3] for protection. Please. I'll call you as soon as I've talked to the doctors."

Becca had left the hospital like a beaten dog.

Would they let Granny go home today? Was the stroke not that bad? She couldn't believe that.

1 toiletries – Hygieneartikel 2 to chuck out – hinauswerfen 3 mattress – Matratze

Exercise 61

Lückenfüller: Ergänze das fehlende Wort in den Sprichwörtern.

1. *to be the ________________ of the walk*
2. *Don't cross your ________________ before you come to them.*
3. *I wouldn't want to be in her ________________.*

Becca thought of all the wonderful holidays she had spent at her Granny's home on the Lizard Peninsula as a child. All their picnics by the beach, their long walks, their games of hide and seek on Granny's little farm, baking apple pie from her own big apple tree in the garden. Lying in the grass and watching the clouds painting animals and funny faces into the sky.

Exercise 62

„Am Lesen sein": Setze die folgenden Verben in die Verlaufsform.

1. *When Ms Dingles came into school, Becca (search) ________________ her desk.*
2. *When Dash arrived at the kiosk, Helen (wait) ________________ for her date.*
3. *When Becca came home in the dark, the blue light (flash) ________________ on the ambulance.*

Even the rainy days had been adventures: they had opened old suitcases[4] of cracked[5] dark leather and cardboard boxes belonging to Granny's parents and grandparents in the attic[6]. Becca could smell the dust and mothballs[7] as she remembered the old costumes. They had dressed up as circus performers who balanced on broomsticks[8] or tamed[9] cushions which were meant to be wild lions and tigers.

Sometimes they had pretended to be old-fashioned couples who walked through the small farmhouse living room like aristocrats in a park. Granny had always had a saying to hand, a habit she had taken over from her own grandmother.

Becca opened the door and walked into her grandmother's room. She sat down on Georgina's bed and inhaled the old lady's smell of sleep, lavender and soap.

Becca could not imagine that her grandmother could go on living without those old sayings if her stroke meant she had lost all her memories. Since she had got Alzheimer's they were her only connection with what she had always been and liked in her life. She had forgotten everything but her sayings. Would Granny lose this anchor to herself now? Would she ever come home?

Becca sighed and started to tear off the bedclothes[10]. This was the only chore[11] Georgina had always insisted on[12] doing herself and Leonora had advised Becca not to talk about it as she had thought it was because of nightly misfortunes[13] that Granny had wanted to cover up[14]. But now Becca saw there was not a single stain on her grandmother's linen[15]. Becca lifted the mattress to examine the underneath[16]. It was immaculate[17].

What had her mother been talking about? Becca decided to turn the mattress. When she lifted it a big brown envelope fell to the floor. She had not seen it before. She sank down on the bed and took the envelope in her hands. It was quite heavy and really thick.

4 suitcase – Koffer 5 cracked – rissig 6 attic – Speicher 7 mothballs – Mottenkugeln 8 broomstick – Besenstiel 9 to tame – zähmen 10 bedclothes – Bettwäsche 11 chore – Hausarbeit 12 to insist on sth. – auf etwas bestehen 13 misfortune – Missgeschick 14 to cover up – verdecken 15 linen – Bettwäsche 16 underneath – Unterseite 17 immaculate – unbefleckt, einwandfrei

Exercise 63

Zeitreise: Setze die Verben in die Zukunftsform (*future*, z.B. *will go*)!

1. *Becca (not forget) ________________ her Grandma's lovely home.*
2. *Georgina (lose) ________________ her memories.*
3. *Leonora's taxi (be destroyed) ________________ if Becca doesn't pay the money.*

Her fingers felt an elevation in the middle, it felt like – money?

Carefully Becca opened the envelope.

Many banknotes were in it. Becca counted four thousand pounds, all in small notes.

Becca's heart widened. It was the same feeling she had experienced in her childhood on Christmas Day unwrapping her presents.

What a surprise!

Becca sank back on Georgina's bed and threw the money up in the air. The notes tumbled down on her body and the bed and floor like leaves in autumn.

After a while Becca's happiness cooled down. She sat up and carefully collected all the banknotes.

Where did Granny get that much money from?

She took a second look into the envelope and pulled a letter out.

The small, even[18] handwriting of her Granny, which Becca knew so well, said:

18 even – hier: gleichmäßig

My dearest daughter and granddaughter
Take this in the unlikely event that I might need care.
"A stitch in time saves nine[19]!"
With love
Georgina

Becca sat still, the letter in one hand, the banknotes in the other. They were trembling.

She stared at the money and one of her Granny's favourite idioms came into her mind:

"Nothing ventured, nothing gained[20]."

Becca slowly nodded.

And started to cry.

19 a stitch in time saves nine – spare in der Zeit, dann hast du in der Not 20 nothing ventured, nothing gained – frisch gewagt ist halb gewonnen

Chapter 27

At 4 p.m. Dash handed the keys for the ferry over to his boss. Andrew took the late shift.

The day had been cooler than the rest of the week and not as many tourists had taken the ferry as usual. Heavy clouds were lingering over the village and Andrew had said the weather would change.

Dash feared this was Andrew's indirect way of telling him that he didn't need Dash any longer. But Dash had not dared to ask. He would come to work as usual until he was told otherwise. But he would keep his eyes open for a new and better opportunity.

Exercise 64

Nicht müssen: Bilde die Verneinung der folgenden Sätze.

1. *Helen had to admit that she had been out at night.*

   ____

2. *Dash had to clean the boat after work.*

   ____

3. *Jack has to make a decision about his profession.*

   ____

He had called Becca several times during the day, but she had either not answered her phone, or she had said she didn't have time to talk. Dash walked along the quay to the beach. He had taken Helen home the night before. All the time he had had a feeling of familiarity[1] about Bono172. He could not work out what it was.

Exercise 65

Besserwisser: Erkläre auf Englisch, was die Sprichwörter bedeuten.

1. *It's no bed of roses.*

   ____

2. *It's six of one and half a dozen of the other.*

   ____

3. *It's a piece of cake.*

   ____

Dash was hoping to find an answer to this question by the bench where Helen had been sitting last night. Maybe the flasher[2] had lost something, maybe all of a sudden Dash would work out what was familiar. He couldn't stop thinking about this and at the same time he had a strange feeling in his guts[3], like somebody was tearing at them.

Although the dark sky kept people from bathing, the lawn in front of the beach and the beach itself were crowded. Parents were building sandcastles with their children, some were playing with beach balls. Two small girls were hitting a ball with cricket bats[4]. The ball kept going in the wrong direction, which made

1 familiarity – Vertrautheit 2 flasher (coll.) – Exhibitionist 3 guts – Eingeweide 4 bat – hier: Schläger

them scream their frustration out loud. It looked funny and many of the watchers on the iron benches by the beach laughed and applauded the girls.

Dash did not laugh. The cricket bats – they were familiar to him. At this thought, out of the blue[5] his former gang appeared from behind the icecream kiosk. When he saw their leader, Dash knew at once what had appeared familiar. Jamie moved from one leg to the other like Bono172 had done the night before. And he was wearing the same black leather shoes, while all the others had trainers on like Dash himself.

"You bloody bastard," Dash hissed and stepped in front of Jamie Dagger. He had a black eye[6] and some bruises on his face. Nevertheless he grinned and showed Dash the middle fingers of both hands.

Dash pushed his hands into his pockets and counted backwards from a hundred to ninety. Only then could he be sure of having his voice under control.

"Stop bullying Helen, Bono172!"

"Ah! So now it is Helen you are protecting? Have you given up on Rebecca? Clever of you to accept it – she's mine now."

"Close your eyes and you will see what is yours. If you carry on like this you'll get another black eye before you realise what's hit you."

"Are you nuts? What are you talking about, little ferryman?" Jamie replied.

The boys behind him were laughing and nodding, so he went on. "Who do you think you are, threatening me? And who the hell is Bono whoever[7]? Can't you see that you are outnumbered[8]?"

"I only see that you are brave when you have your slaves[9] behind you. Don't force me to find out how brave you are when you haven't got company!"

5 out of the blue – aus heiterem Himmel 6 black eye – blaues Auge 7 whoever – wer auch immer 8 to be outnumbered – in Unterzahl sein 9 slave – Sklave

The gang moved forward like one man. Dash focussed on Jamie.

Exercise 66

Besserwisser: Was ist in den folgenden Sätzen richtig, Adjektiv (z.B. *light, good*) oder Adverb (z.B. *lightly, well*)? Setze die richtige Form ein.

1. *Andrew had said the weather would change (slight)* ____________________.
2. *Parents were (silent)* ____________________ *building sandcastles.*
3. *Some people were playing with a (soft)* ____________________ *ball.*

Suddenly the two small girls from the beach came running between them on their way to the icecream kiosk, forcing Jamie and his gang to step back.

Dash took the chance and joined a group of tourists who were going into the harbour office.

Chapter 28

When the final school bell rang, Sandra leaned back in her chair and put her head in her neck. She still had a bad headache. It had been too much for her. Everything.

It was not only the threatening letter and the suspicion[1] that one of her students might have stolen a valuable watch. The burglary last night had appeared to be her biggest challenge. Again she had decided not to call the police, as nothing seemed to have been stolen.

She had checked that last night. But she had to admit to herself that her school's recent situation looked very different from former threats through bad boys' pranks.

One classroom window at the back of the building was broken, but the caretaker[2] had fixed it quickly. Sandra turned the big shard of glass in her hand. She had picked it up last night from the floor. There was blood on it and she could have given it to the police. They could have checked the DNA. And compared it with suspects. If Sandra had had a suspect. And if she had called the police.

If, if, if …

The morning had started with the news that Jack Jacobs was ill and wouldn't be coming. Which was not so bad, as it meant he could not cause any damage. But then Sandra had pondered about his sickness. He had looked quite well the day before. So was he hurt? Had he possibly cut his knee? Could he be the burglar, trying to find out about his personal assessment[3] for his final exam? And the one who had written the threatening letter?

1 suspicion – Verdacht, Argwohn 2 caretaker – Hausmeister 3 personal assessment – persönliche Bewertung

Exercise 67

Satzsalat: Bringe die Wörter in die richtige Reihenfolge!

1. *moved like gang forward the man one.*

   ____

2. *you talking are about what?*

   ____

3. *had convinced he was under that Dash voice his control.*

   ____

The only thing which was remarkable about him was his constant nervousness and lack of talent for his chosen profession. That would support her suspicion. But she had to wait until the young teacher came back – or ask Jennifer Peters if he was limping[4]. She seemed to know Jacobs outside school.

Sandra leaned forward and looked through the notes the secretary had put on her desk during the day.

And Rebecca Higgins. She had to keep her in mind. But at the moment her family had trouble enough, with her grandmother at hospital.

Sandra got up. She had to talk to Ruth, she really needed her sister's advice.

She closed her door, left school and took her car to drive to her sister's. Last night it had been too late.

When she drove up the hill to her sister's house she remembered that Jacobs lived just around the corner.

Later Sandra couldn't tell her sister what made her change her

4to limps– hinken, humpeln

mind not to drive to her sister's place by the direct route but take the side road instead – to get a look at Jacobs' house. But it turned out to be the right decision.

Exercise 68

Wortverdreher: Bilde Fragen aus den folgenden Sätzen, indem du die Wortstellung veränderst und – wo nötig – Wörter ergänzt.

1. *The next morning was sunny.*

   ____

2. *Jack Jacobs was ill the following day.*

   ____

3. *Georgina was feeling better that morning.*

   ____

4. *Leonora was at her mother's side all the time.*

   ____

Sandra put down the sun shield[5] in order to stop herself being seen from the street. And she was lucky.

The young teacher was in his front garden looking up as if checking the weather.

"I would have said I was sick if I had a face like that," Sandra murmured.

He had a bruise on his left cheek, the eye was black and his nose swollen. When he turned around and walked to the front door, he moved slowly. As if his legs were hurt.

5 sun shield – Sonnenblende

Exercise 69

Lückenfüller: Hänge das passende Frageanhängsel (*question tag*, z.B. *You haven't seen her, have you?*) an!

1. *The caretaker had fixed the broken window already,*
   ____________________*?*
2. *The student teacher handed in his sick note,*
   ____________________*?*
3. *Georgina didn't wait for the doctor to come,*
   ____________________*?*

"He must have fallen inside the classroom, right onto his face, through the broken glass pane[6]," Sandra told her sister ten minutes later.

6 glass pane – Glasscheibe

Chapter 29

Becca couldn't make up her mind[1] whether to laugh or to cry. Her Granny's money could save the whole family from ruin and getting hurt. On the one hand.

But on the other hand these were Georgina's savings for a rainy day[2]. How could Becca even think of spending it otherwise, no matter how serious the situation.

When she had finished preparing Granny's bed her mobile phone rang.

Exercise 70

Gewusst, was: Finde die deutschen Entsprechungen für die englischen Sprichwörter (*idioms*).

1. *by using every trick in the book*

   ____

2. *to eat humble pie*

   ____

3. *head over heels*

   ____

"Becca! Finally! What's wrong? Why don't you answer the phone?"

Helen!

1 to make up one's mind – sich entscheiden 2 savings for a rainy day – Notgroschen

"I …" Becca moved her hand over the duvet as if her grandmother was lying under it. There were no words for what she had to say now, but she had to find some. Helen might be the only person she could tell the truth, who would not turn away or call the police.

"I'm so sorry," Becca finally whispered.

"What do you mean, what for?"

"That is – well, Helen, it is a long story. And it is really complicated. Too complicated for the phone. Can we meet? It is important. And maybe dangerous."

At 6 p.m. they met by the Mill Pool behind the amusement arcade. Some families were in the pedal boats[3] on the water. The boats were bobbing up and down[4]. Becca had to stop watching them because her stomach reacted as if she was on one of those boats herself.

Helen shook her head slowly.

"Why didn't you tell me earlier? I would have tried to help you."

"But I did. And you told me you didn't have the money."

Exercise 71

Wessen? Setze die folgenden Sätze in den Genitiv.

1. *Dash bought a cat. The cat is* ________________.
2. *Georgina is in bed. The bed is* ________________.
3. *Jamie took Becca's Jacket. It was then* ________________.

"Yes, that's true. I thought you gave your leather jacket to Jamie Dagger as a present. And I was – well. I was disappointed that

3 pedal boat – Tretboot 4 to bob up and down – auf dem Wasser schaukeln

you lied to me about that. And why you were at the headmistress's office that long."

"I should have told you earlier, I'm sorry."

"It is all about confidence[5] and faith in your friends[6], you know."

"But what can I do now?" Becca stood up from the wall they were sitting on and walked a few steps. "How can I get out of this mess? Do you think I can take my Granny's money – just for now – and pay it back after I've earned it in the holidays?"

"Your Mum doesn't know about the money, you said. Are you sure?"

"Quite sure, yes. Granny always made her bed herself. And if she had told my mother, she would have taken the money to the bank, for safe keeping[7]." Becca rubbed her eyes. They were itching. "But the money – what if Granny needs it right now? She is so poorly. I can't believe they'll let her leave hospital. Mum won't leave her alone for a second, she is really worried, although she's trying to hide it."

Exercise 72

Besserwisser: Liste mindestens 5 Adjektive der Zeit auf.

1. ____________________
2. ____________________
3. ____________________
4. ____________________
5. ____________________

5 confidence – Vertrauen 6 faith in s.o. – Vertrauen auf jmd. 7 safe keeping – sichere Aufbewahrung

Helen watched her all the time and nodded. "I'm so sorry about – well, about everything. But your Granny is the most important thing. And you're right. You can't take her money. And you don't have to. You know, if you pay protection money once you will have to pay it over and over again. That's how blackmail[8] works. They never stop. And you will get deeper and deeper into this mess."

Helen got up and walked close to Becca. She took both Becca's hands and pressed them firmly.

Becca shook her head.

Exercise 73

Parallelwelten: Finde das Gegenteil der aufgelisteten Begriffe und notiere es.

1. *victory* ________________
2. *to admit* ________________
3. *departure* ________________
4. *health* ________________
5. *birth* ________________

"We can't call the police, if that's what you're suggesting. They will arrest[9] me for stealing your mother's wristwatch! And for the burglary at school."

Helen wiped Becca's cheek. It was wet.

"And what if we drive the taxi away so they can't destroy it?" Helen didn't look too convinced by her own suggestion.

Becca shook her head.

8 blackmail – Erpressung 9 to arrest – verhaften, belangen

Exercise 74

Täter und Opfer: Setze die folgenden Sätze in das Passiv.

1. *Jamie beats Becca up.*

   ____

2. *Dash steered the ferry.*

   ____

3. *Ms Dingles called her sisters.*

   ____

"They will come the next day or the day after. They will never stop. As you said!"

Helen pushed her hand into her sides. She had a determined[10] look on her face when she said firmly: "Yes, they will. You are right, the only way to beat these guys is to show them they can't hurt you. We will face those guys, show them that they can't frighten us, that you are not alone. They will stop blackmailing you the very moment they see that you are not alone."

10 determined – entschlossen

Chapter 30

By 9:45 p.m. they were waiting for the gang.

With Becca's house and the taxi right behind them, they were both pretending to look over the grey water towards the dark bird island across the bay.

Exercise 75

Vieles: Setze die folgenden Sätze in den Plural (und zwar alles, was sinnvoll ist).

1. *The boy is using a computer programme.*

   ____

2. *The teacher teaches a student.*

   ____

3. *The student tries to get out of the lesson.*

   ____

Helen was having an icecream with three huge scoops[1]. She was obviously enjoying it, while Becca had already run to the toilet in her house three times within the last fifteen minutes.

Becca jumped up again and walked a few steps in the direction she suspected the gang would come from. Her legs were restless, the skin was itching all over her body. And if she had been on her own she would have scratched herself.

1 scoop – Eiskugel

There were some tourists going into the pub on the opposite side of the road. They were in holiday mood as Becca judged from the laughing and chatting[2] along. She wished she was somewhere else, holidays or not, but not in this lousy place.

How could Helen stay so calm?

Exercise 76

Lückenfüller: Ergänze das fehlende Wort!

1. *Helen didn't look too ________________ at her own suggestion.*
2. *The police will ________________ me for stealing your mother's wristwatch!*
3. *The only ________________ to beat these guys is to show them they can't hurt you.*

Becca had watched her talking on the phone the last time she had come back from the toilet. When Helen had seen her, she had put the mobile away and started licking on her ice cream again. And when Becca had asked whom she had been talking to, Helen had only replied "Mum".

Now she had finished and wiped her mouth with a paper towel.

"There they are," Helen hissed and pointed behind Becca.

The gang was approaching, led by Jamie Dagger as expected. He was holding something long in his hand. The others followed him. They were like one big organism, moving from one side to the other. Their faces looked determined, no smile, no looking away. They knew their aim. It was Becca.

2 to chat – plaudern

Exercise 77

Strippenzieher: Verbinde die folgenden *phrasal verbs* (Verb mit Partikel) mit der richtigen deutschen Übersetzung.

turn in (US-amerikanisch)	*einschalten*
turn down	*umdrehen*
turn on	*abgeben*
turn over	*erscheinen*
turn up	*herunterdrehen*

Becca felt her stomach convulse[3]. She fumbled in her pocket for the money. It was still there, a hard roll of banknotes. Five hundred pounds. Held together by a rubber band. Helen does not need to know that.

Jamie stopped in front of Becca. The long item in his hand was a cricket bat.

Becca swallowed. Jamie looked strange with his sunglasses on, she had never seen him wear those before. And he had her jacket on again.

Jamie pulled up one corner of his mouth into a half-grin that made him look ugly and dangerous. He started to swing his bat gently. This movement was taken up by his mates. There were five of them, all with baseball or cricket bats in their hands, moving them to and fro[4] like the tentacles of a giant octopus.

Exercise 78

Hauptsache: Unterstreiche die Substantive (keine Namen!) im vorigen Absatz und setze sie in den Plural oder Singular.

3 to convulse – zusammenkrampfen 4 to and fro – hin und her

Becca stepped back until her buttocks[5] hit the bench. Then Helen was at her side and grabbed her hand.

"Hi guys," Helen said. Becca was surprised at how strong Helen's voice could be.

"Looking for trouble tonight?" Helen went on. "You can find it here, if you plough ahead[6]!"

Becca tried to breathe slowly to get rid of the little black spots which were dancing around in front of her eyes. Her heart was racing. She squeezed Helen's hand firmly. Her other hand was still in her jeans pocket closed around the banknotes.

Exercise 79

„Am Lesen sein": Setze die Verben in den folgenden Sätzen in die Verlaufsform.

1. *Becca (read) ________________ a book.*
2. *Dash (worked) ________________ in the harbour.*
3. *The ships (lay) ________________ on their sides.*

"We are here for the money, Rebecca. Didn't you want your jacket back? This is your chance ..."

Becca looked at Jamie. She couldn't see his eyes. She shook her head. "I haven't got the money."

"And you should go and look for a job, if you need money," Helen said and included[7] all the others in her advice with a gesture of her hand.

"As you've done all your life, Lady of the Hills?" Jamie replied. Now he had a dark grin on his face. He looked back over his shoulder and nodded towards the others. They walked behind

5 buttocks – Hinterteil 6 to plough ahead – weitermachen 7 to include – einschließen

Becca and now they stood close to her mother's car, to her family's only source of income[8].

Exercise 80

Lückenfüller: Setze die richtigen Präpositionen ein!

1. *When Becca had asked whom Helen had been talking ________________, Helen had only replied "Mum".*
2. *Jamie pulled ________________ one corner of his mouth.*
3. *You will find trouble if you plough ________________.*

"No!" Becca exclaimed and pulled her hand out of Helen's. She leaned against the car and stretched out her arms over the passenger's door protectively.

"No, please. My grandmother ..."

Jamie laughed out loud.

"Are you trying to convince[9] me with your grandmother?"

He looked around. Becca followed his gaze. There were no tourists around at the moment. The other gang members had realised that too. The guy with the curly[10] red hair lifted his baseball bat quickly and smashed it on the engine bonnet[11]. It came down with a loud bang[12] and left a long dent[13], a deep scar in her mother's car.

Becca jumped aside. Helen caught her, kept Becca from falling.

Then they heard a strong voice from behind.

"Here comes trouble ..."

8 source of income – Einkommensquelle 9 to convince – überzeugen 10 curly – lockig 11 engine bonnet – Motorhaube 12 bang – Knall 13 dent – Delle

Exercise 81

Betrüger: Welche der folgenden Aussagen ist falsch?

1. *Jamie is the leader of the gang.*
2. *The others follow him without thinking.*
3. *Dash is still one of them.*

Chapter 31

Dash hurried up the walkway and was out of breath when he reached the crime scene. Becca was in Helen's arms and that stupid red-haired Fisher was slamming his bat onto Becca's mother's car.

Exercise 82

Buchstabensalat: Sortiere die Buchstaben so, dass sinnvolle Wörter entstehen!

1. *venomemt* ________________
2. *angusdero* ________________
3. *wakywal* ________________

Dash had to attract their attention[1] to stop them from destroying the taxi.

"Here comes trouble, Jamie Dagger," he cried, and stopped in front of the gang leader.

"Still not looking good today?" He pointed at Jamie's sunglasses.

"You'd better watch your step or this ...," Dash made a dramatic overarching[2] movement with both arms, "... will all end up badly[3]."

The gang members collected behind Jamie, only Fisher remained by the car. He looked so stupidly and with such a funny expression of pride[4] at the dent he had produced that Dash had to laugh out loud.

1 to attract s.o.'s attention – jemandes Aufmerksamkeit erregen 2 overarching – allumfassend 3 to end up badly – ein schlechtes Ende finden 4 pride – Stolz

Exercise 83

Zukunftsmusik: Bilde die Zukunftsform, die eine feste Absicht ausdrückt oder unmittelbar bevorsteht (mit *going to*).

1. *Becca (gives) ________________ Jamie her Grandma's money.*
2. *Dash (fights) ________________ the whole gang.*
3. *Helen (protects) ________________ Becca and the taxi from the gang.*

Jamie frowned. He waved his guys to come closer.

"You bloody[5] traitor[6]! How dare you laugh at me?"

Dash moved one step closer to his opponent[7]. At least he had drawn their attraction away from the girls and the car.

"You will never find out how strong you really are, Jamie Dagger, if you don't meet somebody on your own," he hissed and felt the tension between his shoulders.

Exercise 84

Fundstücke: Finde im vorhergehenden Kapitel die englischen Entsprechungen zu diesen Sätzen und unterstreiche sie.

1. *Wir sind wegen des Geldes hier.*
2. *In dem Moment waren keine Touristen zu sehen.*
3. *Dann hörten sie eine starke Stimme hinter sich.*

5 bloody (coll.) – verdammt 6 traitor – Verräter 7 opponent – Gegner

Jamie made a pointing movement with his head and Garner, the biggest guy in the gang, stepped forward in front of Jamie and lifted his fists against Dash.

"You still can't fight for yourself, can you, you loser?" Dash said to Jamie, without letting the tall guy out of his focus. He concentrated on tensing[8] his belly muscles.

But when the blow hit him in the middle, the pain almost knocked him off his feet. Dash stumbled backwards and clenched his teeth. Jamie would not hear a sound of pain from him. Dash shook his head to get the exploding stars out of his sight and the pulsating pain in his guts under control.

Garner stood frozen as if surprised that Dash was still standing. His gaze changed from surprised to questioning when Dash pulled himself up to his full height as if nothing had happened. Garner turned to Jamie waiting for further instructions.

Exercise 85

Zeitreise: Setze die Verben in den folgenden Sätzen ins Präsenz.

1. *The harbour (was) ________________ deserted at this time of the day.*
2. *The school caretaker (repaired) ________________ the window.*
3. *The student (ran) ________________ home after school.*

Dash looked at his watch. He had known how this would end. So where the hell were they? He didn't want to be turned into these guys' punchball!

8 to tense (muscles) – (Muskeln) anspannen

The girls were still by the taxi. He was sure they would not leave. Becca had covered her eyes with her hands and was sobbing. Helen stood at her side, patting her shoulder. But she looked at Dash. And he could see concern in her eyes.

When Garner ducked in front of Dash to prepare the next blow Helen shouted "No!" and ran towards Jamie as if she wanted to fight him.

Exercise 86

Satzsalat: Bringe die Wörter in die richtige Reihenfolge!

1. *known this end he how had would.*
2. *tensing concentrated muscles his on he.*
3. *his Jamie waved come to closer mates.*

"Go away!" Dash shouted and moved forward, pushing Garner. But he was strong as a wall, repelling[9] Dash's fists as if they were flies.

And then Dash heard the police siren.

9 to repel – abwehren

Chapter 32

"So it's decided," Ms Dingles said, and Becca's mother nodded.

"Rebecca?" Ms Dingles focussed on her and Becca finally had to say something.

Helen, who was sitting in a chair right next to Becca, dug her in the side with her elbow.

Exercise 87

Vieles: Bilde den Plural der folgenden Substantive!

1. *crash* ____________________
2. *bus* ____________________
3. *church* ____________________

"Yes, okay, decided. I'll work in the nursing home where they will send Granny to recover after her hospital treatment."

Ms Dingles leaned back behind her desk and seemed satisfied[1].

But Becca's mother did not.

"And you will not report the … Rebecca's attempt to … take the watch from your office?"

"Well, I think Rebecca has been sufficiently[2] punished with the development of events," the headmistress said to Becca's mother. Then she turned to Becca. "You know, Rebecca, that gang went far beyond bad boys' pranks. What they did to you was a crime, a serious crime. And if it wasn't for[3] Dashiel

1 satisfied – zufrieden 2 sufficiently – ausreichend 3 if it wasn't for s.b. – wenn jmd. nicht gewesen wäre

Hunter the damage[4] would have been much greater. You two might have got hurt. Now the police will take care of those guys and they will get what they deserve. And it will be a lot more comfortable[5] in our little village without them, I can tell you. So, young lady, next time you get into trouble you should tell a grown-up earlier."

Exercise 88

Zeitreise: Setze die Verben in die einfache Vergangenheit (*past tense*, z. B. *went*)!

1. *Dash pushes Jamie and hopes for help.*

   ____

2. *Becca regrets what she has done.*

   ____

3. *Leonora can't believe what Becca has done.*

   ____

Ms Dingles looked at Helen and back at Becca. Becca's mother was sitting in her chair without moving. Her eyes were red from lack of sleep and crying over her daughter ever since the police had taken Becca to hospital the previous[6] night. Becca hadn't had much sleep herself. She had stayed there all night, until her mother had taken her to school this morning.

Ms Dingles had not yet finished.

4 damage – Schaden 5 comfortable – hier: sicher 6 previous – vorhergehend

Exercise 89

Betrüger: Finde die falsche Übersetzung des Sprichwortes.

to bark up the wrong tree	*den falschen Baum anbellen*
Beggars can't be choosers.	*In der Not schmeckt jedes Brot.*
to bite the bullet	*in den sauren Apfel beißen*

"I know you don't want to hear it now, but we have more experience and know what needs to be done. If you had told your mum the day they beat you up and took your leather jacket away you could have saved yourself a lot of worry and wrong turns."

Becca nodded. And after a long pause she said: "But the threatening letter – it wasn't from me."

"No, dear, I know that already."

Helen sat up. "Then who wrote it?"

"That is really not something you two need to know!" Ms Dingles gestured that Becca and Helen could leave.

Exercise 90

Parallelwelten: Finde die Gegenteilpaare und verbinde sie mit Strichen.

discourage	*sad*
enter	*separate*
glad	*freeze*
join	*encourage*
melt	*exit*

The last words Becca could hear through the door from Ms Dingles were: "Your daughter was a victim first and foremost. And an offender[7] only as a result. But please keep an eye on her, as soon as your mother is better and back home from hospital. Rebecca needs you too."

7 offender – Täter

Chapter 33

Sandra Dingles went to the secretary's office and got herself a cup of coffee. She needed it after last night at her sister's place. She had stayed late, but in the end Ruth had told her that she only had to wait until the young teacher found out himself that he was on the wrong track with his vocation[1]. Sandra was willing to follow this advice.

Exercise 91

Besserwisser: Liste mindestens fünf Adjektive auf, die Formen umschreiben.

1. ____________________
2. ____________________
3. ____________________
4. ____________________
5. ____________________

The police visit early this morning about her two students and the fight last night had opened her eyes to the reality about what she had thought were only bad boys' pranks. She really needed to be more alert[2].

The meeting with the girls and Rebecca's mother had been her last big task for the day, Sandra was hoping.

The secretary's voice caught her attention.

1 vocation – Berufung 2 alert – aufmerksam, wachsam

Exercise 92

Setze die passenden Wörter (und nur die) aus der folgenden Liste in die Sätze ein.
sister, routine, victim, sister's, problem, offender

1. *Ms Dingles had stayed late at her* ________________ *place last night.*
2. *Your daughter was a* ________________ *first and foremost.*
3. *Becca's* ________________ *is of a financial and ethical kind.*

"Ah, Ms Dingles, Jay … sorry, Mr Jacobs dropped in just to hand in his sick note. He looked like a boxer – his face was all swollen. The note is from Dr Martin, the dentist[3]. I bet he's had an operation. My son looked the same after the extraction of his wisdom teeth."

So the dentist has taken the last tiny piece of wisdom from this unlucky man, Sandra thought.

Exercise 93

Betrüger: Welche der folgenden Aussagen ist falsch?

1. *Becca's mother was not amused, but she was not too angry.*
2. *Ms Dingles told Becca and Helen who had written the threatening letter.*
3. *Jack Jacobs was not at school this morning.*

3 dentist – Zahnarzt

She had to talk to him. Maybe she could make him change his mind about becoming a teacher. Everybody needed a second chance and the option to take a new start. As Rebecca's mother had done when her husband had left her alone with her daughter and mother.

Tough woman, Sandra thought, how she deals with all the stress in her life. And now this new challenge with her daughter, her mother not yet over the hump[4]. But Rebecca has inherited her mother's toughness. She only has to find the right way to prove it. But the last few days will help her.

4 to be over the hump – über den Berg sein

Chapter 34

After he had delivered his sick note at the school office Jack went back home and took a painkiller. He hung up his coat and turned towards the desk. The puddle of red ink on the desk was still there. It had dried and looked as if somebody had shot himself sitting there. The dead body had been removed.

Exercise 94

Lückenfüller: Setze die richtigen Präpositionen ein!

1. *Keep an eye ________________ Becca, she needs you.*
2. *Ms Dingles wants Jack to change his mind ________________ becoming a teacher.*
3. *Jack had a tooth extracted ________________ his jaw.*

Jack took a deep breath. The red puddle admonished[1] him that he could not go on like this. His mother's symbol of fulfillment of duties[2] was lying in the middle of the red stain, broken. But his will was not.

The wound from the extracted tooth was really painful, but the dentist had said it would get better soon. He got back into his bed, pulled the cover over himself and thought about how to tell his parents about his new plans.

When he had gone out the night before he had first taken the road to school. He had had the vague idea of stealing the test the headmistress had taken from him. But then he had seen a light in

1 to admonish – ermahnen 2 fulfillment of duties – Pflichterfüllung

her office. And imagined her working all night. He had not hesitated for a second, but turned around and walked away from the school. And at that moment he had known that being a teacher would never be his aim, working day and night at school.

Exercise 95

Betrüger: Finde die falsche Übersetzung des Sprichwortes.

to clear the air	*reinen Tisch machen*
All good things come in threes.	*Aller guten Dinge sind drei.*
April showers bring May flowers.	*Alles neu macht der Mai.*
to compare apples and oranges	*Äpfel und Orangen vergleichen*

He was fed up with covering his lack of knowledge and his exam nerves[3]. He had already committed a crime by sending the threatening letter.

Exercise 96

Verbbeuger: Ergänze die fehlenden Konjunktionsformen der folgenden Verben (z. B. *go, went, gone*)!

1. *arise,* ____________, ____________
2. *eat,* ____________, ____________
3. *forget,* ____________, ____________

3 exam nerves – Prüfungsangst

Jack pulled the cover over his face. He could only hope the headmistress would not undertake further investigations about the letter. That would be too embarrassing for him! And what if his parents ever heard about this attempt to evade[4] what was only a demonstration lesson[5], after all?

Jack sat up.

What was wrong with him?

He was 26 years old, had no profession, no girlfriend and no idea on how to go on living. The only thing he knew for sure was that he would never become a teacher.

Jack started laughing. The painkiller was working. His mother's pen was gone. He was far away from his parents' place.

He was only 26 years old! He was in lovely Cornwall! His life was waiting for him!

Jack sat up in bed and took out his laptop.

He opened a new text document and typed "Resignation[6]".

4 to evade – ausweichen 5 demonstration lesson – Lehrprobe 6 resignation – Kündigung

Chapter 35

On their way over the Looe bridge Helen took her mother's wristwatch out of her bag. "How can a simple watch be so valuable?" she asked and looked into Becca's face.

Becca shrugged her shoulders[1]. She had been surprised that the headmistress had handed Helen the watch. Becca had expected she would be exposed to Helen's mother as a thief. That had been the most frightening part of her fears when she had tried to get to sleep in the uncomfortable seats in the waiting area of the hospital.

Exercise 97

Besserwisser: Was ist in den folgenden Sätzen richtig, Adjektiv (z.B. *light, good*) oder Adverb (z.B. *lightly, well*)? Setze die richtige Form ein.

1. *Helen had a (light) ________________ suntan already.*
2. *Becca was suffering (bad) ________________.*
3. *Georgina did not make a (quick) ________________ recovery.*

Her mother had refused to leave when Georgina had to undergo surgery[2]. Last night had been the critical time. But at 7 a.m. the surgeon[3] had come and told them Georgina would live and recover. Maybe not fully, but a lot.

What is an embarrassing[4] exposure in comparison to Granny's situation? Not much, Becca admitted, not much. Especially when you deserve it.

1 to shrug one's shoulders – mit den Schultern zucken 2 to undergo surgery – operiert werden 3 surgeon – Chirurg 4 embarrassing – peinlich

"Shall I come and explain it to your mum?" Becca asked when they had crossed the bridge and their ways were about to part[5].

"Well, I would be more interested in how you managed to get this watch …"

And Becca stopped, cleared her throat and started speaking.

5 to part – sich trennen, auseinandergehen

Chapter 36

When Becca began her account with the words: "Can you remember that sunny day last week?" the scenery unfolded before Helen's eyes like a movie.

It was one of those rare days in Cornwall when all day not a single cloud covered the deep blue sky and when the surface of the sea looked like a mirror.

Becca and Helen walked along the beach in the late afternoon, collecting shells and pebbles which looked like small gems[1]. The stones felt smooth and good in their palms. They had left their trainers by the steps at the bottom of the cliffs and walked with their feet in the water. The waves were mild and the water didn't feel as cold as usual.

Exercise 98

Wortverdreher: Bilde Fragen aus den folgenden Sätzen, indem du die Wortstellung veränderst und – wo nötig – Wörter ergänzt.

1. *The sky was blue in the afternoon.*

   ____

2. *The harbour was crowded in summer.*

   ____

3. *The ferry owner liked Dash.*

   ____

1 gem – Edelstein

Helen felt happy and full of pleasant anticipation about going on the internet to chat with Bono172 again. But, looking back now, she also remembered a weird sense of aggression in Becca.

Helen had skipped stones over the water, a habit which was quite childish, but they both liked it and it had become a habit the previous summer. They enjoyed this stone skipping competition: the winner with the most skips got an icecream cone from Helen's parents' freezer afterwards, the loser got one as a consolation prize[2].

On that day, Becca did not join Helen in the competition as she had done a hundred times before.

On that day Becca stepped aside, took a shoebox-sized rock and threw it into the water with both hands. As if she wanted to kill a fish. And she did not stop after the first stone. Becca threw rocks into the water until Helen laughed.

Helen had not taken this behaviour seriously that day, but now she understood that Becca had been under great pressure.

Exercise 99

Fundstücke: Finde im Anfang des Kapitels die englischen Entsprechungen zu diesen Sätzen und unterstreiche sie.

1. *Die Szene entfaltete sich vor Helens Augen wie ein Film.*
2. *Die Steine fühlten sich in ihren Handflächen glatt und gut an.*
3. *Helen hatte kleine flache Steine über das Wasser geworfen.*

Becca had turned around suddenly and walked back to the steps, waving at Helen to follow her.

2 consolation prize – Trostpreis

"Let's go and help your mum in the greenhouse," Becca shouted as she ran up the steep steps. And Helen ran after her, not understanding why Becca preferred[3] the hot greenhouse to the clear air and mild wind outside.

Later Helen's mother had explained to her that Becca was attracted by everything she did not know from her own experience in her family, like the large house, the surroundings, the greenhouse and the conservatory.

On that bright day Helen's mother wanted to pot flowers in containers. Their housekeeper Nora had brought them in from the patio. Helen's mother was very pleased when Becca asked if she could help.

"Have you seen my gardening gloves, Helen?" her mother asked. Helen and Becca helped her look, but they couldn't find the gloves. And finally Helen's mother shrugged her shoulders and took off her wristwatch.

Exercise 100

Liste alle Adjektive des Geschmacks auf, die dir einfallen.

Helen did not notice where she put it. She stayed in the conservatory and checked her e-mails for Bono's reply.

Becca worked side by side with Helen's mother.

Later on Becca carried the finished containers back to the patio, although Helen's mother said that Nora could do it later on. Helen's mother was so happy about the unexpected help that she forgot to admonish Helen about her excessive use of the PC.

3 to prefer sth. – etwas vorziehen

Chapter 37

Becca finished her story with the words: "Well, I noticed where your mother put her wristwatch, between the containers. And I took it. I'm so ashamed. If you'll let me I'll come with you and explain everything to your mother."

"Why should you come?" Helen replied. "This afternoon I'll find this watch in the conservatory, as you did. Only this time it will have fallen from the table and I found it in one of the orchids' pots. That's it!"

Exercise 101

Parallelwelten: Finde die Gegenteilpaare und verbinde sie mit Strichen.

messy	*wealth*
near	*closed*
in front	*far*
open	*neat*
poverty	*behind*

Helen smiled and rubbed Becca's arm.

"Relax. Everything will be fine."

That was … Becca didn't find the right words.

"Thank you, Helen, you are a real friend."

"Good to know, hm?"

"Yes. And Dash." Becca bit on her lips. "How did he know we needed help?"

"He saved me from that Jamie Dagger when he flashed at me last night. And he told me that he was concerned about you, how you had changed." Helen looked away. "Yes, we talked about you. And I trusted him and called him on the phone last night."

Becca closed her eyes. She had been so blind about Dash, blinded by her Granny's saying "Birds of a feather flock together[1]". She should have known better, should have understood that Dash was different from his former gang!

"And where is he now?"

Helen looked down at her trainers[2]. "He is having his first day on a fishing boat today, full contract. Dash is very proud."

Becca felt a sting[3] in her heart.

"And why do you know that and I don't?"

"Well, Becca, can't you figure that out for yourself?"

"So …" Becca hesitated. "So Dash is your boyfriend now?" Becca could hardly hold back her tears.

Helen touched Becca's elbow softly. "Why don't we meet him tonight when he's finished work and talk about everything?"

When Becca passed the little church on her way home she stopped and walked in. She was all alone in the chapel.

But she didn't feel alone, she felt a lot better than she had over the previous few days.

Helen didn't have to explain it to Becca, she had learned her lesson. Her Granny's saying "Better safe than sorry!"[4] did not apply to friendship and love.

Mistrust is a one-way street. And confidence causes confidence.

1 birds of a feather flock together – gleich und gleich gesellt sich gern 2 trainers – Turnschuhe 3 sting – Stich, stechender Schmerz 4 better safe than sorry – Vertrauen ist gut, Kontrolle ist besser

And although Becca knew that even if not everything was fine right at the moment, she was not alone. The most important thing was to have people who cared. About her Granny, about her mother, about her friends and about herself.

Final Quiz

1. *Where does the story take place and what do you know about that area?*
2. *What do you know about Rebecca's family? How does she live?*
3. *What does Rebecca's mother do for a living?*
4. *Becca's grandmother is suffering from a disease. Do you know the name and what it means?*
5. *Is there anything that can be done to calm Becca's granny down when she gets excited?*
6. *How does Helen live?*
7. *What do you know about Helen's parents?*
8. *Who is Dash and what does he want?*
9. *What does Jamie want from Becca and what has he already done to her?*
10. *Jamie threatens to do something really bad if he doesn't get what he wants from Becca. What is it? And what would it mean for Becca's family?*

Answer Key To The Exercises

Exercise 1:	1. write, 2. leave, 3. read
Exercise 2:	1. the headmistress's , 2. the children's, 3. her house's
Exercise 3:	1. children, 2. information, 3. teachers
Exercise 4:	She tapped the letter with her finger.
Exercise 5:	In for a penny, in for a pound. Wer A sagt, muss auch B sagen. All good things come in threes. Aller guten Dinge sind drei. to make ends meet sich nach der Decke strecken
Exercise 6:	1. better, best, 2. worse, worst, 3. lighter, lightest
Exercise 7:	1. knew, 2. was, 3. liked
Exercise 8:	1. admit-deny, 2. annoy-please, 3. below-above
Exercise 9:	1. into, 2. on, 3. out
Exercise 10:	1. educational, 2. hobbyhorse, 3. scholarship
Exercise 11:	1. has gone, 2. has stopped, 3. has fallen
Exercise 12:	3. muss heißen: der Hahn im Korb sein
Exercise 13:	1. will cancel, 2. will call, 3. will face
Exercise 14:	3. Becca stayed where she was.
Exercise 15:	1. lay, lain 2. sat, sat, 3. hung, hung
Exercise 16:	1. body, 2. back, 3. dozing
Exercise 17:	3. Jack is the student teacher.
Exercise 18:	steps-step, boat-boats, rope-ropes, ferryman-ferrymen, hand-hands, handrail-handrails
Exercise 19:	1. hair – mir standen die Haare zu Berge, 2. shoes – ich möchte nicht in ihrer Haut stecken, 3. old – das ist ein alter Hut/kalter Kaffee

Exercise 20:	look up	nachschlagen
	look forward	sich freuen
	look for	suchen
	fall out	sich streiten/ausfallen
	get across	verdeutlichen

Exercise 21: 1. were looking, 2. was chasing, 3. was keeping

Exercise 22: 1. will kid, 2. will be, 3. will go out

Exercise 23: do, did, done; stop, stopped, stopped; ask, asked, asked; have, had, had; search, searched, searched; be, was/were, been; look, looked, looked; will, would, would; call, called, called

Exercise 24: 1. Becca is not able to pay the money. 2. Helen is not allowed to go to the festival on her own. 3. The old lady is not able to climb the steps faster.

Exercise 25: 1. Dash is going to start the boat's engine. 2. Ms Dingles is going to inform Becca's mother.
3. Helen is going to take care of Becca's problems.

Exercise 26: 1. would leave, 2. would like, 3. would move

Exercise 27: 1. Helen must/may not leave the school. 2. Ms Dingles must/may not talk about the threatening letter. 3. Dash must/may not show he is annoyed.

Exercise 28: 1. The teachers don't have to search the students.
2. The students don't have to show them their backpacks. 3. The headmistress doesn't have to report the threatening letter.

Exercise 29: 1. must/has to, 2. must/have to, 3. must/has to

Exercise 30: 1. to be on cloud nine – auf Wolke sieben schweben – überglücklich sein, 2. The apple doesn't fall far from the tree. – Der Apfel fällt nicht weit vom Stamm. – Wie der Vater, so der Sohn,
3. to sail close to the wind – kurz vor dem Chaos stehen

Exercise 31: 1. She heard her own voice tremble. 2. Becca moved quickly down the stairs. 3. How are your bruises today?

Exercise 32: 1. angry, 2. angrily, 3. frightfully

Exercise 33: 1. Did Ms Dingles suspect Becca of being a thief? 2. Did Dash want to get a proper job? 3. Did Jamie blackmail Becca for money?

Exercise 34: 1. do you, 2. didn't you, 3. can I

Exercise 35: Don't cross your bridges before you come to them.
Kümmere dich nicht um ungelegte Eier.
to take coals to Newcastle
Eulen nach Athen tragen
Don't toot your own horn.
Eigenlob stinkt.

Exercise 36: 1. Becca's mother takes her hand and strokes it like a cat. 2. Helen switches her mobile on again. 3. Georgina wants to go to the circus.

Exercise 37: 1. the young lady's backpack, 2. the harbour's/ harbour entrance, 3. the mouse's hole

Exercise 38: 1. It was hot inside the conservatory. 2. The lawn in front of the house looked like a putting green. 3. The water looked like a mirror.

Exercise 39: 1. trees, 2. bees, 3. advice

Exercise 40: 1. friendlier, friendliest, 2. more wonderful, most wonderful, 3. more seldom, most seldom

Exercise 41: 1. wanted, 2. worried, 3. suffered

Exercise 42: smooth-rough, deep-shallow, many-few, weak-strong, cheap-expensive

Exercise 43: 1. at, 2. forward, 3. about

Exercise 44: Richtig muss es heißen: 2. When she was about to dial Helen's number …

Exercise 45: 2 ist eindeutig richtig.

Exercise 46: 1. thunderstorm, 2. celebration, 3. disappointment

Exercise 47:

active	lazy
alike	different
borrow	lend
cloudy	clear
courage	cowardice

Exercise 48: 1. has gone, 2. has left, 3. has prepared

Exercise 49: That's not your cup of tea – heißt: Das ist nicht dein Ding.

Exercise 50: 1. His jaw muscles relaxed a bit. At least enough for him to speak. 2. Which had made the others laugh and take the mickey out of him. 3. Their lack of willingness to think for themselves had always repelled Dash.

Exercise 51: 1. wasn't he, 2. hadn't he, 3. did she

Exercise 52: rush, rushed, rushed; come, came, come; insist, insisted, insisted; leave, left, left; have, had, had; get, got, got; take, took, taken; dial, dialled, dialled

Exercise 53: 1. Is Helen allowed to go out at night on her own? 2. Is Ms Dingles allowed to chuck out the student teacher Jack easily? 3. Is Becca able to smash the window pane with a rock?

Exercise 54: 1. will withdraw, 2. will be, 3. will not achieve

Exercise 55: 1. Becca may/must not break into her school. 2. Teachers must/may not be unfair. 3. Georgina may/must not remain alone.

Exercise 56: 1. bind, bound; 2. blow, blew; 3. drink, drunk

Exercise 57: 2 ist falsch: Georgina was at home when Becca left the house at night.

Exercise 58: figure-figures, office-offices, light-lights, intruder-intruders, window-windows

Exercise 59: 1. closing, 2. poured, 3. understand

Exercise 60:	keep away	(sich) fernhalten
	keep up	weitermachen
	look out	aufpassen
	look for	suchen
	put off	verschieben

Exercise 61: 1. cock, 2. bridges, 3. shoes

Exercise 62: 1. was searching, 2. was waiting, 3. was flashing

Exercise 63: 1. will not forget, 2. will lose, 3. will be destroyed

Exercise 64: 1. Helen didn't have to admit that she had been out at night. 2. Dash didn't have to clean the boat after work. 3. Jack doesn't have to make a decision about his profession.

Exercise 65: 1. It's not easy. 2. It doesn't make any difference/ Both people in an argument are equally right, or equally wrong. 3. It's easy.

Exercise 66: 1. slightly, 2. silently, 3. soft

Exercise 67: 1. The gang moved forward like one man. 2. What are you talking about? 3. Dash was convinced that he had his voice under control.

Exercise 68: 1. Was the next morning sunny? 2. Was Jack Jacobs ill the following day? 3. Was Georgina feeling better that morning? 4. Was Leonora at her mother's side all the time?

Exercise 69: 1. hadn't he, 2. didn't he, 3. did she?

Exercise 70: 1. nach allen Regeln der Kunst, 2. zu Kreuze kriechen/kleine Brötchen backen, 3. Hals über Kopf

Exercise 71: 1. Dash's, 2. Georgina's, 3. Jamie's

Exercise 72: Mögliche Antworten: old, young, late, early, ancient, fast, long, modern

Exercise 73: 1. victory-defeat, 2. to admit-to deny, 3. departure-arrival, 4. health-illness, 5. birth-death

Exercise 74:	1. Becca is beaten up by Jamie. 2. The ferry is steered by Dash. 3. Ms Dingles' sister was called by Ms Dingles.
Exercise 75:	1. The boys are using computer programmes. 2. The teachers teach (some) students. 3. The students try to get out of the lessons.
Exercise 76:	1. convinced, 2. arrest, 3. way
Exercise 77:	turn in — abgeben turn down — herunterdrehen turn on — einschalten turn over — umdrehen turn up — erscheinen
Exercise 78:	corner-corners, mouth-mouths, half-grin-half-grins, bat-bats, movement-movements, mates-mate, bats-bat, hands-hand, tentacles-tentacle, octopus-octopuses
Exercise 79:	1. is/was reading, 2. was working, 3. were lying
Exercise 80:	1. to, 2. up, 3. ahead
Exercise 81:	3 ist falsch: Dash gehört nicht mehr zur Gang.
Exercise 82:	1. movement, 2. dangerous, 3. walkway
Exercise 83:	1. is going to give, 2. is going to fight, 3. is going to protect
Exercise 84:	1. We are here for the money. 2. There were no tourists around at the moment. 3. Then they heard a strong voice from behind.
Exercise 85:	1. is, 2. repairs, 3. runs
Exercise 86:	1. He had known how this would end. 2. He concentrated on tensing his muscles. 3. Jamie waved his mates to come closer.
Exercise 87:	1. crashes, 2. buses, 3. churches
Exercise 88:	1. Dash pushed Jamie and hoped for help. 2. Becca regretted what she had done. 3. Leonora couldn't believe what Becca had done.

Exercise 89:	Die deutsche Entsprechung für "to bark up the wrong tree" ist „auf dem Holzweg sein"	
Exercise 90:	discourage	encourage
	enter	exit
	glad	sad
	join	separate
	melt	freeze
Exercise 91:	Mögliche Antworten: broad, flat, skinny, crooked, curved, deep, hollow, low, narrow, round …	
Exercise 92:	1. sister's, 2. victim, 3. problem	
Exercise 93:	2 ist falsch: Ms Dingels hat nicht verraten, wer den Brief geschrieben hat.	
Exercise 94:	1. on, 2. about, 3. from	
Exercise 95:	"To compare apples and oranges" wird im Deutschen zu „Äpfel mit Birnen vergleichen".	
Exercise 96:	1. arose, arisen, 2. ate, eaten, 3. forgot, forgotten	
Exercise 97:	1. light, 2. badly, 3. quick	
Exercise 98:	1. Was the sky blue in the afternoon? 2. Was the harbour crowded in summer? 3. Did the ferry owner like Dash?	
Exercise 99:	1. The scenery unfolded before Helen's eyes like a movie. 2. The stones felt smooth and good in their palms. 3. Helen had thrown small flat stones over the water.	
Exercise 100:	bitter, sweet, salty, fresh, hot, sticky, icy, fresh, prickly, strong, soft, tasteless, yummy	
Exercise 101:	messy	neat
	near	far
	in front	behind
	open	closed
	poverty	wealth

FINAL QUIZ: SOLUTIONS

1. The story takes place in Looe in Cornwall. It is a town which is divided by the Looe River, which dries up at low tide. It is a touristy place in summertime, but deserted in winter.

2. Becca's father left the family some time ago. Becca lives together with her mother Leonora and with Leonora's mother Georgina.

3. Leonora owns and drives a taxi.

4. Georgina suffers from the Alzheimer's disease, a disease which leads to forgetfulness. Only the long-term memory keeps working for a while.

5. Yes, Georgina comes from an old circus family and she can still remember the old days. She likes wild animals. If you tell her about the animals in her imaginary circus she calms down.

6. Helen lives in a big house on the cliffs. There is direct access to a beach, palm trees and a conservatory.

7. Helen's parents are wealthy and enjoy going to the theatre.

8. Dash is Becca's boyfriend. He used to be one of the bad boys but has changed and is looking for a job to earn his living and to do something useful.

9. Jamie wants money from Becca. He has already beaten her up and taken her leather jacket.

10. Jamie threatens to damage Becca's mother's taxi, which would mean the family would lose their source of income.